CW01080342

INCREDIBLE DIARY OF...

Worlds Of Adventure

Edited By Jenni Harrison

First published in Great Britain in 2023 by:

Young Writers
Remus House
Coltsfoot Drive
Peterborough
PE2 9BF
Telephone: 01733 890066
Website: www.youngwriters.co.uk

All Rights Reserved
Book Design by Ashley Janson
© Copyright Contributors 2023
Softback ISBN 978-1-80459-666-1

Printed and bound in the UK by BookPrintingUK
Website: www.bookprintinguk.com
YB0549A

FOREWORD

Dear Diary,

You will never guess what I did today! Shall I tell you? Some primary school pupils wrote some diary entries and I got to read them, and they were EXCELLENT!

Here at Young Writers we created some bright and funky worksheets along with fun and fabulous (and free) resources to help spark ideas and get inspiration flowing. And it clearly worked because WOW!! I can't believe the adventures I've been reading about. Real people, make believe people, dogs and unicorns, even objects like pencils all feature and these diaries all have one thing in common – they are JAM-PACKED with imagination, all squeezed into 100 words!

Here at Young Writers we want to pass our love of the written word onto the next generation and what better way to do that than to celebrate their writing by publishing it in a book! It sets their work free from homework books and notepads and puts it where it deserves to be – **OUT IN THE WORLD!**

Each awesome author in this book should be super proud of themselves, and now they've got proof of their imagination, their ideas and their creativity in black and white, to look back on in years to come!

CONTENTS

Collingham Lady Elizabeth Hastings CE Aided Primary School, Collingham

Dottie Bolton (11)   61
Skye Mizen (11)   62
Delilah Potter (10)   63
Millie Murgatroyd (10)   64
Sophie Townley (11)   65
Nell Pickersgill (10)   66
Sophie Bailey (10)   67
Eidy Johnson (10)   68
Sophie Fraser (11)   69
Austin Reeve (10)   70
Annie Penrose (11)   71
William Driver (11)   72
Teddy Smitherman (11)   73
Lauren Jayne McAllister (11)   74

Elmwood School, Rushall

M G (11)   75
Rebecca Spendlove (11)   76
Josie Evans (11)   77
Charlie Smyth (11)   78
Jon Jones (11)   79
R-Jay Manby (11)   80
Riley Cabrera (12)   81
Junior Stansbie (11)   82
Harry-Lee (11)   83
Rhys Sheamar (11)   84
Simon Smith (11)   85

Northlands Primary School And Nursery, Pitsea

Arike Shokanmbi (11)   86
Amelia Vernazza (11)   87
Daniel Arthur (11)   88
Edwardine Nimoh-Ababio (11)   89
Sophie Tressider (10)   90
Terrence Turner (7)   91
Olley Ricci (10)   92
Nancy Bleu (10)   93

Jessica Perry (9)   94
Keeon Downes (11)   95
Geremi Rous (11)   96
Ella Tice (10)   97
Lola-Belle Philip (11)   98
Jessica Broom (9)   99
Amelia Lefever (11)   100
Owuraku Asiedu (8)   101
Zuzanna Adamska (10)   102
Raylan Hewlett (11)   103
Tommy Hayhoe (11)   104
Jack Hodges (11)   105
Chloe Wincott (9)   106
Yara Yousf (10)   107
Ollie White (10)   108
Ellie Sartin (10)   109
Lily-Rose Knight (10)   110
Georgie Bennett (10)   111
Abbie Gregson (10)   112
Agata Odinas (11)   113
Lewis Morrell (10)   114
Logan Gardiner (11)   115
Elliot Adom (9)   116
Julia Sikora (11)   117
Tegan Down (11)   118
Kai Harrison (10)   119
Siena Wallace   120
Halle Adams (8)   121
Yanel Senour (11)   122
Layla Atherton (11)   123
George Costen (11)   124
Samuel Olatunji (10)   125
Alessia Garril (10)   126
Camelia Aioanei (11)   127
Jayden Andah (10)   128
Gabriel Sava (8)   129
Anthony Atiase (7)   130
Ruby Nichols (10)   131
David Radulescu (10)   132
Zunaira Chowdhury (10)   133
Jack Carter (9)   134
Zachary Hayward (9)   135
Alaina O'Sullivan (11)   136

Qanita Owolabi (7)	137
Summer Nenada (10)	138
Jayden Hall (10)	139
Millie Tomlin (11)	140
Khloe McKay (10)	141
Mohab Abdalla (10)	142
Katie Sweeney (10)	143
Nathaniel Hayward (11)	144
Riley Bryant (9)	145
Ana Serbu (9)	146
Annabelle Wood (9)	147
Jake Oliver (10)	148
Betsy Gordon (10)	149
Rhayan Parker (10)	150
Kacey Foster (10)	151
Sophie Waldron Brown (10)	152
Amber Merchant (10)	153
Antonia Atiase (7)	154
Anya Muthuthamby (11)	155
Ruby Pammen (9)	156
Elle-Jade Anderson (10)	157
Gracie Oliver (9)	158
Meshach Ngoma Minzako (9)	159
Archie Green (9)	160
Skye Sayer (10)	161
Clay Bainbridge (11)	162
Roman Oliver (10)	163
Faith (10)	164
Gracie-Lee Read (10)	165
Jacob-James Sculley (10)	166
Caleb Eastwood (10)	167
Sid Butler (10)	168
Gabriel Atiase (10)	169
Nikolas Tunase (9)	170
Casey Harding (10)	171
Izzie Hibbitt	172
Ramsey McDala (10)	173
Jude Jones (10)	174
Catriel Heredia Aguiar (10)	175

Shrewsbury Cathedral Catholic Primary School, Castlefields

Fenella Lambert (11)	176
Liepa Petrenaite (7)	177
Lacee Beau Fairley (8)	178
Martha Reavey (11)	179
Oluwadamilola Grace Osewa (10)	180
Isabell Abraham (11)	181
Vimbai Mhembere (8)	182
Ayansh Raneesh (7)	183
Oluwatimileyin Osewa (7)	184
Jacob White (8)	185

Southfields Primary School, Stanground

Temidayo Oladipupo (11)	186
Zayaan Hammad (5)	187
Aisha Keita	188
Mazin Elmahi (11)	189
Hanika Padmanabhan (9)	190
Krithvik Sankaranarayanan (7)	191
Caris Isaac (10)	192
Mariama Embalo (9)	193
Yatika Prabhuram (7)	194
Alex Ivanov (9)	195
Briony Hill (8)	196
James Logan (7)	197
Oliver Traynor-England (11)	198
Maisie Palmer (7)	199
Ratika Prabhuram (7)	200
Wiktoria Nowak (11)	201
Amelia Wlodarczak (8)	202
Poppy Whittington (6)	203
Isobel Bishop (9)	204
Eila Reeves (8)	205
Brooke Bell (8)	206

The Boy Who Went To Space

Dear Diary,

Once I went to space, so I know what you're thinking, "You really went to space as a kid?" Yes, I did go. In fact, my whole family went. It was awesome. We fought angry aliens, ate cool space cheese and drank succulent spaceonade.

Suddenly, the rocket hit something. *Crash* went the rocket.

"What was that?" I shouted.

"It was a humongous asteroid," said the pilot.

"A humongous asteroid?" I cried. "What are we doing to do?" I said.

"I have no idea," said the pilot. He breathed in and quickly demolished the asteroid. We all cheered, "Yay!"

Tara Wintoki (8)

Benedict House Preparatory School, Sidcup

A Soldier In Space

Bang! Bang! Soldiers were dropping like flies. It was incredibly intense that my heart skipped a beat. Oh no, the aliens were raiding our base. We all panicked and were running around like headless chickens. The enemies acquired a part of our base.

"Open up!" The aliens had breached our security and now were banging on our metal doors.

"Get down! They're breaking in!" *Bang!* They busted our door down and now we had to fight back. They blasted their sophisticated weapons and destroyed our entire crew. Except for me. What will happen now? Will I be everlastingly doomed?

Michael Abounu (11)

Benedict House Preparatory School, Sidcup

The Sneaky Sneak (AKA The Sneaky Panda)

In the jungle, a sneaky panda lived there. One day, he wanted his mum's phone. He crossed the jaguar, the wolves, the cheetahs, the big humongous elephant until he got to his dad's house. He stopped. He ate dinner in the shed. They ate fresh bamboo. His dad asked, "Do you have Mummy's phone yet?"

"No." And he carried on walking. When he got to his mum's house he grabbed her phone.

Whilst sneaking out, "Hey, that's my phone, I didn't give you permission! Give it back you cheeky," said Mummy.

"Oh man, seriously? I wanted to play some games."

Aviela Akintunde (8)
Benedict House Preparatory School, Sidcup

World War Pizza

Dear Diary,
We've just met pineapple pizzas and even looking at them is enough to declare war! Fruit and pizza should not exist! Technically tomatoes are fruit, but it is still sickening to even think about! Actually, that's just what we'll do: we will declare war. We'll fight them to the death and if it's still not enough, we'll throw them in the microwave! I forgot to mention, the pineapples quoted: "Pepperoni and pizza is revolting!"
This is enough. I have to declare war against them! I'm worried they will fight back! Hopefully, I can get a good night's sleep.

Vito Daniele (11)

Benedict House Preparatory School, Sidcup

Squirtle's Forest Adventure

Dear Diary,

This sunny, bright day, I, Squirtle, the creature that has a smooth shell and shiny blue skin, walked through a marvellous forest.

Suddenly, some people came over and said, "You pesky, smelly creature. Get out of the way. Shoo!" I didn't want to listen to these unkind strangers, ruining my day, so I aimed my water shooters at their bodies and *kaboom!* They disappeared into the beautiful sky. Smiling to myself, I felt protected by my powers. Later that afternoon, I met a crowd of funny-looking creatures who I made friends with. What a strange day that was!

Leo Ryan (8)

Benedict House Preparatory School, Sidcup

Buddy Who Goes To Pup Academy

Once there was a pup called Buddy and he was strolling outside when his human had left for school. He fell and hit a hole in a tree and went through it and landed in another world. He was wearing a uniform. Then a big dog came along and shouted, "Head to class!"

"Okay," he said. They learned a lot in class. It was nearly break. *Ring! Ring!* Break.

"Oh look, there's a wood. Let's go in!"

"Wow!"

"Oh no, we are lost!"

The teachers were looking everywhere until they found them. They had fallen asleep in the forest.

Keira Christina Folan (8)

Benedict House Preparatory School, Sidcup

Poor Pencil

There I was minding my own business, having a lovely sleep, when the ground started to shake around me. Everyone knows what that means! It means it's the start of school! The friends rushed to their seats ready for another day of school. I heard the teacher announce, "We're writing stories today!"

"No," I said to myself, "more pain!" A brute grabbed me and started brushing my head against some paper. Then he dropped me on the floor. That really hurt. They picked me up and rubbed my head against the paper again! Just like every normal day. It's painful.

Henry Frost (10)

Benedict House Preparatory School, Sidcup

Teacher Or Evil Mastermind?

Dear Diary,
Yesterday was an overload of madness, and it all began when I was attempting to solve a complex maths equation. Our teacher (Mr Jefford) was teaching us division, which I found very challenging. It was whilst working that I noticed my teacher kept writing in his crimson journal. Unsure what he was logging, I pondered all the possibilities. Then, after class, I opened his drawers and identified the subject. I then looked at what he had been scrawling curiously. Taken by surprise, I deciphered the title, 'Taking over the world'. Could my teacher be an... evil mastermind?

Jessica Churchill (11)
Benedict House Preparatory School, Sidcup

Prettiest Pig In The World

Just another normal day at Porkey Farm. I was rolling around in my muddy puddle when I noticed Miss Lavender with shimmering lipstick on. Oh, how I wished I could sparkle like her! I must have said this out loud as George Pig trotted over, whispering, "Let's hatch a plan."

George had lived in the farmhouse as a little piglet. He showed me a secret tunnel that went straight into Miss Lavender's bedroom. I helped myself to the brightest, pinkest, piggiest lipstick I could find. It was perfect! I felt more glamorous already and I'd only just got started!

Annabelle Wise (8)

Benedict House Preparatory School, Sidcup

The Man Who Went To Space

Jack went to space but never came back. He went without his diary. Some kind aliens came down to Earth to record his activities in his diary.

They returned to space to show him the diary and their terrible writing. But they noticed that Jack, the astronaut, had sadly passed away because he didn't have food nor water for forty-five days.

The aliens were so sad that they destroyed the moon, just to bury him.

They informed Jack's family who were devastated to hear the news. Jack's family took him out of space and buried him properly on Earth.

Zane Eze (8)

Benedict House Preparatory School, Sidcup

Chair

Dear Diary,

Today was relentlessly tiring. First, at noon, I got squished by an obese person (it was pain-filling!), hours felt like days, even weeks! Luckily, nobody would disturb me for a prolonged time, but that wretched beast came back! Would this be longer? No! People were going up and down. One guy had his disgusting feet on me and was rocking around, left, right, all around. It was unsurprisingly overwhelming. Only a couple of minutes passed and I felt nothing, smelled nothing and had it felt good? Yes! Wonderful, I loved it. Until the obese beast came back!

Finlay Sansom (11)
Benedict House Preparatory School, Sidcup

Stuck On The Moon

Dear Diary,

My trip was terrible. I got stuck on the moon! A vicious creature broke my ship with his claws! They were after the supplies, all I had was one sandwich. The sandwich was the flavour I hated most; watermelon, jam, cream, water and dust. Then I saw the creature, it had three heads, and two noses (I don't know where the other nose went). It had vicious claws and devilish hair which was dusty reddish. The vicious machine looked at me. He took my sandwich. I shouted, "Give it back, you horrible creature!" The horrible creature attacked me...

Ashwin Mann (11)

Benedict House Preparatory School, Sidcup

The Diary Of A Piano

Dear Diary,

I woke up and my back was aching because yesterday there were lots of people prodding me. Whenever my keys got touched, a peculiar sound came out. I'm used to it now. *Thud! Smash! Boom! Wham! Crash! Slam!* I was certainly sure that they weren't playing me right because the racket that came out wasn't pleasant. I looked up and saw two young faces peering at me whilst smirking. I couldn't tell them to stop because I can't speak, but the last noises were *Thud! Thud!* It was like they knew I was trying to say help me!

Abigail Lamina (10)

Benedict House Preparatory School, Sidcup

Pizza Wars

Dear Diary,

Today my best friend Simon ordered pizza! My favourite pizza ever! It had: gooey cheese, fresh tomato sauce and crispy pieces of pepperoni. Simon and I gobbled all of it up until there was one slice left. Pizza was my favourite so of course I grabbed it. Simon glared at me from across the room. This meant war!

Within seconds, I started shouting at him saying I deserved it because I went to the terrifying gym three weeks ago! Instead of being the better person, he said he went last week! Suddenly, my wife said, "Just halve it!"

Sophia Smidmore (11)

Benedict House Preparatory School, Sidcup

The Dog Space Invader

Dear Diary,

My humans were busy this morning, but Mum's slippers looked so good! I only gave them a little chew... Mum saw me and screamed, "Go outside you naughty dog." I hung my head in shame and trotted into the garden. Suddenly, a passing spaceship scooped me up. It was full of food. The aliens loved collecting Earth food and had felt sorry for me. Well, I began eating everything. They became angry with me too! They pushed me out and I landed back in my garden, thankfully, my jelly-filled belly helped me bounce. What a great day!

Sarah Rosser (8)

Benedict House Preparatory School, Sidcup

Turning Into A Queen

There I was, staring straight in front of me. Looking at the space I could be promoted into, the gracious, glorious and most importantly, free queen! Never again will I be doomed to move in the same direction with seldom occasions of moving one space diagonally, taking a piece or initiating en passant. So basically useless. Although I do like it when I capture blundered and hanged pieces. Maybe I don't want to be a queen anymore. It was too late. The player grabbed me and advanced forwards. I was a queen. Yay! I was seized right after. No! Defeat.

Oluwademilade Wintobi (10)

Benedict House Preparatory School, Sidcup

Chilli Productions

Dear Diary,

I started a job. It would be splendid I thought - it was not. I am a respectable adhesive toy not a piece of junk. I arrived at 'Chilli Productions' (makes sense as I am in that form). When I arrived, two humans came and turned my spicy energy into fuel for a bomb! Then they tested my power by hurling me against human number two in a bomb shelter. This happened several times until I was worn out. Afterwards, they threw me at the ceiling! Now, I am stuck there. Being sticky and a 'toy' chilli is terrible!

Palash Dasgupta (11)
Benedict House Preparatory School, Sidcup

The Day I Met Coco

Dear Diary,

What an exciting day! Today, after school, my parents surprised me with the most amazing gift ever (and I don't mean sweets!). I met the cutest, cuddliest most adorable Cavapoo and her name is Coco. Coco is very energetic and she loves to explore. She is so friendly, I just know we will have lots of adventures together. But first I need to train her. It is not easy to get a cheeky puppy to listen to instructions. Some dogs I've seen in the park can do tricks. But I would be happy if she stopped chewing slippers!

William Wright (7)

Benedict House Preparatory School, Sidcup

My Apple Farm

Yesterday, I went to the farm to collect some apples. But before I got my second apple, a boy named Tom took my apple. I was so angry that I could throw the apple tree at him, but I couldn't because he was throwing all the apples at me! I jumped into the car and we drove as fast as we could, but the boy was faster. He was still throwing the apples until my mum stopped the car, got out and said, "I'm reporting you to your father!"
Tom pleaded, "Please, please don't tell my parents. I will stop!"

Tiwalola Olabode (8)
Benedict House Preparatory School, Sidcup

A Diary Of An Amazing Cat

I can't believe it, I've been in the pet shop for a whole week! I'm like the prettiest cat in the world! One day, a bald man came into the shop. He looked quite strange and then he asked the pet man to buy me. I was excited to go to my new home. On the way, he told me his plan to destroy the world. Soon, we got back to his secret lair but then we heard a voice. "You!" said my dad, "You are not getting away this time!"

"Oh yes I am, you idiot!"

"Into the piranhas!"

Eden Chidgey-Robertson (8)
Benedict House Preparatory School, Sidcup

Chick-Napped!

Dear Diary,

I was given a chick. I named it Goldie. At lunchtime, I allowed her outside to run around, when a fox kidnapped her! I was very concerned since she was my first pet. When I went outside again, for one last look, I discovered a chirp from behind the shed. Warily, I stepped over the vines to the back of the shed.

Where is she? I thought. I was taken aback when I saw my beloved pet! Ever so gently, I scooped her up as she chirped in delight. Next time, I won't abandon her outside alone.

Amelia Hussain (11)
Benedict House Preparatory School, Sidcup

The Incredible Diary Of A Basketball

Dear Diary,
I have had a truly incredible day today. First, I was taken to a room where I was filled up with air. Next, I was taken to a room with many Homo sapiens enclosing and staring at me. All of a sudden, I was bounced on the ground painfully, several times. It hurt. As soon as the pain wore off, they started bouncing me again! This time, they did it ceaselessly. Hours passed as I kept getting bounced. After a while, I felt like I couldn't move anymore. Surprisingly, after the game, they abandoned me!

Raghav Subbiah (10)
Benedict House Preparatory School, Sidcup

The Brussels Sprouts

Dear Diary,

We are always left alone on a plate and never eaten. Until yesterday somebody actually ate one of us! We were shocked. No one has ever devoured one of us! Suddenly, he started grabbing us. Of course I was one of the lucky sprouts to still be alive - being able to write this. When Joe, (yes that's his name) eats Brussels sprouts, only a few would be left on the plate and the rest usually eaten (of course not all of them are eaten). Did I forget to mention, my name is Harry. Will I be eaten next?

Dylan Compston (10)

Benedict House Preparatory School, Sidcup

The Girl Who Had Superpowers

Yesterday I found out that I had superpowers. It started at school yesterday when my friends and me walked in the field after school and that was where I got my superpowers. Me and my friends were chatting about pets and all of a sudden my hands were tingling and my head felt dizzy. Before I could say help me, I was up in the air! I could fly. I zoomed and my friends were amazed and there were going to tell my parents but I said, "Don't tell my parents. They will freak out. Just help me please girls."

Elsa-Grace Waigo (8)

Benedict House Preparatory School, Sidcup

The Diary Of My Hairband

Dear Diary,

Today she used me in the most uncomfortable style on Earth. The dreaded half up, half down. What felt like fifty hours passed, finally it was time to be put down. But of course, tragedy struck; I was tangled in her knotted brunette hair. I was thinking nothing else could compare to being stuck... I was wrong! She cut me! I thought it was over, but no. She tied me back together. It was soooo good to know I could be used again. Little did I know that would be my final hairstyle. The awful half-up.

Edie Dobson (10)
Benedict House Preparatory School, Sidcup

The Shoe

Today, I had the worst day. I was having a calm and peaceful thirty seconds of my life, until... *Bash!* That's going to bruise tomorrow. I smelt a nasty smell. "Argh!" A human slipped their rancid foot into me! We walked out of the house and I was drenched. We arrived at school safely. I spoke too soon. "Oh my gosh!" I felt something squelch against me. I felt like crying. I had a tough day. I'm sure tomorrow will be no different. Every day will be painful to remember.

Dharam Marwaha (11)

Benedict House Preparatory School, Sidcup

The Firework Show

Dear Diary,

I'd arrived at what was a firework light show. The screaming of children, tasty aroma of food and the piercing bang of fireworks were on my mind. I knew what I was doing first, and that was to wait in a vast line for food. After a while, I finally achieved my hot dog. My dad advised me to go on the tallest ride to get a good view, high in the cold air. *Bang!* The firework flew up in the air. A sizzle appeared in the sky and exploded. Days have to end and this did too.

Aarav Kunwar (11)

Benedict House Preparatory School, Sidcup

Hermione Had The Best Day

Dear Diary,

Yesterday I found out that I was a wizard. It all started at home when I was eating lunch with my family. I saw something weird. I went to the doorway and I saw a wand. I was surprised to see a random wand at my door. I grabbed it and showed my parents. They looked shocked and told me to put it back so instead of putting it back, I pretended to and took it to my room.

The next day I saw an owl on me. I shouted. My parents came and said, "What happened Hermione?"

Taushini Katragadda (8)

Benedict House Preparatory School, Sidcup

The Stick

Dear Diary,

Today was a painful day. I got picked up by this old guy, then I got thrown to an unknown area. I had this animal chase me like I'm some kind of toy. I got stepped on, chewed on, and even peed on! I was all wet by the time it was done. But little did I know what was coming next. I got picked up by the same animal's mouth and was brought back to that old guy and got thrown again. It kept repeating on and on. Today was really one painful and tiring day!

Amariah Oriri (11)

Benedict House Preparatory School, Sidcup

The Miner Finding The Orb

One day, there was a miner who was obsessed with finding this magical orb. He already searched like a billion caves but he never gave up on finding the magical orb that he had searched for in the magical cave. He searched far and wide. It was really hard for the miner to look in every cave. He searched and finally found the magical orb. He felt ecstatic. He had finally found the orb. This was the best time of his life. He felt really proud of himself.

Vivin Vinothkumar (8)

Benedict House Preparatory School, Sidcup

The Man In Space

This story is about a man who went to space on his second trip but he never came back. An alien saw the man and treated him to his home. He wanted to go back home. He was too scared to stay in space. So a kind alien helped. They were so close but his spaceship broke down so they rang a fixer. The alien fixed the ship and they went back on their trip to Earth. They got closer but they ran out of fuel so they rang the fuel alien and he fixed the ship.

Jeevan Purewal (8)
Benedict House Preparatory School, Sidcup

Burning Trees Down

Dear Diary,

Today I accidentally burned two trees down. I had a little cold so I sneezed a flame on my morning walk. It hit my trainer but he didn't care because Quaxly blew the fire out. We had to pay a bill for the damage. I felt a little sorry for my trainer. Have I told you about Quaxly? Oh, sorry. He is my brother. His nickname is Timothy. He likes spraying water around but not near me! I hope my cold will go away by tomorrow.

Jonathan Wong (8)

Benedict House Preparatory School, Sidcup

Katie Is Going To Ballet School

Dear Diary,

I was in my room getting ready for ballet school. I had my tutu on and my leotard on and my point shoes in my wee bag. My wee bag was fluffy and soft.

"Katie."

"Yes, Mum."

"Get in the car."

"Okay, Mum."

I walked down the stairs to the car.

"Mum, can we put some good songs on please?"

"Okay, fine."

Five minutes later, we were there.

"Bye-bye Mum."

"Bye-bye sweety. Love you."

"Love you too."

"Hi teacher."

"Hi Katie, how are you?"

"I am good."

Time to do some ballet. Brava arms, plié!"

Katie Burns (10)

Carnegie Primary School, Dunfermline

The Boy Who Bent The Universe

Dear Diary,
The year is 2000. I don't like 2000. I went downstairs for breakfast and overheard Mum and Dad chatting in the kitchen. They were talking about how to travel through different times using a toy.
I grabbed one of my toys and Mum's computer, Dad's rock and a box. I got Mum's computer and plugged it in. I put Dad's rock in the box and the last thing I put in the box was the toy. I climbed inside the box. *Click! Boom!*
"Bob?"
"Yeah Mum?"
"You're alive, you're home." I was home.

Rhys Kinsella (10)
Carnegie Primary School, Dunfermline

My First Match For Dunfermline

Dear Diary,

It's my first game for Dunfermline. I am really nervous. I have loved Dunfermline since I was four years old. I am twenty now.

After I got dressed, I hopped over to the stadium as I stay close. Two minutes later, I got there.

"Oi gaff, where am I playing?"

"Up front!"

"Okay then."

I saw O'Hara. "Hi," I said.

"What's up in the sky?"

After that, it was time to go in the first minute. They scored in the 80th minute. I scored. "Yesss! What a game!"

Leighton Hempseed (10)

Carnegie Primary School, Dunfermline

The Moon

Dear Diary,
My spaceship just crashed on the moon. I'm going out to assess the damage. I'm starting to get worried. The ship's bad and the moon has aliens, I think. The back of the ship is destroyed and my spacesuit too. I've got some oxygen so I can breathe in space. It's awful.
Getting dark now, and all the aliens come out. They are real. I thought they were a myth. I'm definitely feeling sick now. Time to battle it out...
Fast forward ten years, I'm in an alien prison. Been here ten years. They caught me pretty fast.

Lucy Smart (10)
Carnegie Primary School, Dunfermline

Super Fam

Dear Diary,

I'm an ordinary kid. I have an ordinary sister, an ordinary dad and an ordinary mum. We all like TV (like ordinary people). We all like dogs (obviously) but there is a teensy, weensy, tiny, small detail. We are all sups. Not trying to brag but I have the best superhero powers ever. I have laser eyes, the power of flight, regeneration, forcefield, teleportation, time-hopping power and the best of all... Drum roll, please. The power of invisibility and extra. But sadly, I have to keep this all from my friends. Stay tuned for part two.

Scarlett Fraser (10)
Carnegie Primary School, Dunfermline

Aliens Invade The Earth On My 11th Birthday

Dear Diary,
Today Earth got invaded by aliens. It was scary.
Let me explain. So the air-raid sirens went off and
then we ran to the nearest shelter. Next thing you
know, aliens' UFOs are covering the sky and the
aliens pushed but the armies pushed them into
space again. That's how I survived an alien attack.
Except there were more aliens disguised as
humans and they sneakily attacked so we pushed
them out again.
I'm super glad I survived that attack because it's
my 11th birthday and I wanted to live till at least
one hundred.

Adam Heywood (10)
Carnegie Primary School, Dunfermline

The Story Of LeBron James

Dear Diary,

In the first place, Michael Jordan was the best basketball player in the whole wide world. But then LeBron James took his place as champion by beating him in a basketball ball match. Then he became the best basketball player in the whole wide world. He beat lots and lots of basketball players like me, Niko, and other basketball players. I trained and trained and trained until I become good at basketball. Then, I went to the basketball stadium to beat LeBron James and guess who won the match? The beast, Niko.

Niko D'Abbraccio (10)
Carnegie Primary School, Dunfermline

My Discovery

Dear Diary,
On Monday, I was sitting in class looking out the window, wondering what happened to dinosaurs. After school, I was walking my way home, when I saw a bone. I rushed home and went into my lab where I studied stuff. After years of research, I discovered that this bone was once a T-rex. I introduced it to the whole world and became famous. Some people even called me a genius. My parents would treat me as special. I was different now. I was famous. I was really proud of myself and everyone told me I should be.

Hafsa Kamran (10)
Carnegie Primary School, Dunfermline

My First Day At School

Dear Diary,

It was my first day of school. I was so happy. I was in my uniform. When I got there, I saw all my friends. In my head I thought *another year at Carnegie*. The bell went. Only me and my friends were there.

My teacher opened the door. The class looked magic. I stepped in it. It was scary. When I was in, it looked the same. Nothing different. But the class was not there. My teacher said, "Come in class." They had all shown up.

Later we all went home. I loved the best day ever.

Rose Martin (10)
Carnegie Primary School, Dunfermline

Banana Inc

Dear Diary,
Today I got lots of bananas. Here's what happened. I was running through the vents of Banana Inc. My plan was to find the banana room. Suddenly, there was a creak and I fell through the vent into the banana room. Landing like a monkey, because I am a monkey, I planted a tracker on it (I had a tracker!) and there was a deep rumble and a monkey burst through the door. I walked out, hopped into the banana car and drove home. Skidded to the driveway, walked through my door, turned on the TV and slept.

Benjamin Smart

Carnegie Primary School, Dunfermline

Dr Monkey Steals Bananas

Dear Diary,

On Sunday morning, me and the monkeys woke up hungry for bananas. But there were none in our bit of the jungle. Then Doctor Monkey woke up hungry too and he looked angry at my direction. He screamed at us, "Go find the bananas!" So we did. We started to raid the jungle's bananas and took them away from the other monkeys. We then brought them home to Dr Monkey. But he wanted more. So we went to a village. We snuck the bananas and ran with them. We got home safely and Dr Monkey was happy.

Caeden Gartshore (10)

Carnegie Primary School, Dunfermline

The Incredible Supergirl

Dear Diary,
Yesterday was the best day of my life.
This is what happened: I was done with my work so I went into the playground. I was racing with my friend and before I knew it... *Thud!* I was on the ground just like that. I tripped over a magical wand. I turned it with no doubt it would work... It was dark. It was silent and I was wearing a cape. My friend was gone. I went out. I felt like I was levitating. I started to instantly fly. Was I dreaming? This was amazing! I was incredible!

Mariam Irshad (10)
Carnegie Primary School, Dunfermline

The Rock Of Monkey

Dear Diary,

I just had the best holiday of my life. First we got on the plane to Gibraltar from Edinburgh. Then I landed in Gibraltar. I was so excited to see the Rock of Gibraltar.

As I went to the airport shop, I saw a monkey! Then another 20 minutes passed and it was like the monkey army came. All of the monkeys came down from the rock and took an entire gigantic crate of bananas. Oh no! So we stayed one night and went back to good old Scotland. So I went back happy and excited for more.

Jamie Baxter (10)

Carnegie Primary School, Dunfermline

Lost Treasure

Dear Diary,
There was a girl called Carley. Hi, I'm Carley. This is the story of my crazy life. I live in a jungle. The jungle is called 'The Jungle of Bunnies'. Yes, I know, what a weird name. But anyway, today I am going on an adventure to find the stolen monkey banana from the Monkey King.
Okay, so I have arrived at the towers. Hmm. Oh look, there is a button. Let's press it. Oh my God, there it is. Hmm, ooh, there is a rock. Let's try and get it now. 3, 2, 1. Yes!

Carley Knapman (10)
Carnegie Primary School, Dunfermline

My Morning Routine

Dear Diary,

I am waiting on the bus so I will tell you about my morning. I woke up at 6:30am, made my bed and let Bounty out. I went to get pancakes. *Sizzle.* After, I got dressed, let Bounty in and got ready. By 8am, I was taking Bounty on a walk. *Clip!* "Ruff!" By the time I got home, I was getting my sandwich, crisps and fruit. I said to my mum I was going to the gym after school. So I packed my bag and double brushed my hair and said my goodbyes to go.

Darcie Vyrva (10)
Carnegie Primary School, Dunfermline

The Footballer

Dear Diary,
A knocking on my door. *Knock. Knock.* They looked familiar but I'd never seen him before. He said, "Come with me." I didn't trust him. I went in his car and he told me his name but that was it. His name was Max. We went to a football pitch. He got the ball from the back off the pitch and hit it hard and broke the net by how powerful it was. A match began. I was confused. From everywhere, he was scoring. It was boring, no one wanted to play football now.

Ben Carcary (10)
Carnegie Primary School, Dunfermline

Dramatic Day

Dear Diary,

It has been another dramatic day with my bully, Samantha! And today I was just sitting in class when she pulled my hair! (She sits behind me). Then she just laughed it off! Then, at lunch, I was just walking over to my table when she tripped me up! She is so rude. So when she was in the bathroom, I stole her phone. After she came from the bathroom, she was looking for her phone. She was screaming and crying. So I gave it back and she was screaming at me! The day was almost over.

Sophie Kerr (10)
Carnegie Primary School, Dunfermline

The Secret Sceptre

Dear Diary,

I'm in space with a magic sceptre and if you're confused, here's what happened. Let me tell you. It was a normal day and I was in my garden. Later that day, I found a button so I pressed it and a rocket appeared. So I went inside and the rocket launched to space and I saw a planet so I landed. And on the planet, I saw a cave. So I went in and I saw beautiful crystals and at the end of the cave, there was a beautiful golden sceptre. I grabbed it without knowing.

Ben Moran (10)

Carnegie Primary School, Dunfermline

Florida

Dear Diary,

After the long car ride, we finally arrived. I was so excited but I was so hot! When I explored the house, I had an amazing room. It was Mickey Mouse themed. I really liked it. Me and my family got changed into shorts and T-shirts and started to unpack. I was excited to go into the cold pool. Next, we went out to get lunch. We went to a store called 'Walmart'. We got crisps and rolls. We drove home and got into the nice cold pool and ate our yummy lunch. It was so good!

Grace Davidson (10)

Carnegie Primary School, Dunfermline

World Cup 2022

Dear Diary,

I woke up on a bright day. I was going to the World Cup final! I dressed up in my Argentina kit with Messi on the back. I left the hotel to go to the stadium. It was massive! I got VIP seats so close to Messi. So an Argentinian player got the ball and... Goal! Argentina were 1-0 up! Then, Di Maria got tripped in the box. Penalty! Messi ran up to the ball and scored! 2-0! But after halftime, Mbappé got two goals. Then, Argentina won the World Cup and Messi was happy!

Sulaiman Shakil (10)

Carnegie Primary School, Dunfermline

Kung Fu Kally

Dear Diary,

Yesterday I went to school to meet my friend but it was no ordinary day. The bell went, *ring!* First class was science, with my friend Kung Fu Kally. My teacher Miss Summers gave us a three-page workbook. Kally's face got red. *Bang!* She flipped the table and ripped the workbook in half. I hate workbooks. That is not all. At lunch, there were no chips so Kally screamed, "Give me chips!" So she got what she wanted. But that's not all...

Olivia Baillie (10)
Carnegie Primary School, Dunfermline

Trip To Egypt

Dear Diary,

I woke up to the sound of my loud alarm clock, feeling tired and lazy. I had to get up anyway because I was going to Egypt. As soon as I realised that, I was jumping with joy and leapt down the stairs for breakfast. I could never be more excited in my life.

When I landed in Egypt, I felt most excited. After all, I was going to have the time of my life. After I checked into the hotel, I went to step inside a pyramid and fell into a hole. I was never seen again.

Chloe Hedges (10)

Carnegie Primary School, Dunfermline

Moving Miya

Dear Diary

I've moved so many times, I wouldn't be able to count. I first moved when I was four days old and after that I moved when I was 1 and 2 months old. We just moved a couple of days ago to Tokyo, Japan. And now my dad's boss has fired him so now we're running low on money. I'm so scared but then my mom phoned me and I told her everything and my mom came back. She worked non-stop and by six months, we got an apartment and my dad got another job.

Jessica Reid (10)
Carnegie Primary School, Dunfermline

The Greatest Game

Dear Diary,

One day, I was chilling in the house. Suddenly, I heard a rumble. Then I was in a field. It was superbly amazing to play. Then the game started. Then, by halftime, it was 4-0 to City so we needed a miracle to get back from that.

After the break, we were all pumped up to get back but after twenty-nine minutes it was 4-3 after me scoring three. And in the 85th minute, it was 4-4. So in the last second, we scored so we won the game and lifted the cup.

Jayden Guild (10)
Carnegie Primary School, Dunfermline

The Nightmare

Dear Diary,

It was 11:01pm. I couldn't sleep. I was playing on my phone when I got a message from my sister telling me to go to bed and turn the light off because she could see it. So I turned the light off and fell asleep.

I heard a big bang! I woke up. I was in this old broken house. I saw something move in the distance. I saw a black figure. I tried to ignore it but it kept moving closer. I closed my eyes. I woke up in my bed, in my house.

Ava McGovern (10)

Carnegie Primary School, Dunfermline

Planet Pluto

Dear Diary,
This helped unlock a new side of me. This day will forever change me. First, it was like any other work day but it was about to change. I put on my astronaut suit. I took a deep breath and then I went into the rocket. There, I was ready for lift-off. Three, two, one. Lift-off! I felt my heart drop as soon as I left the Earth but the rocket went past Pluto and that was where I was going to land. I turned and I was the first person on Pluto.

Brendan Barber (10)
Carnegie Primary School, Dunfermline

The Boy Who Went To The Moon

Dear Diary,

Today I went to the moon and had a wonderful time. It was amazing. First, I packed and left. I was thrilled so as I left, I ate my lunch and went in the car. Then went to the space station. Once I was there, I put on the puffy spacesuit and went on the rocket ship and headed up! It was a two-hour trip to the moon. Once we landed, the zero gravity was amazing but it was so hot! My trip to the moon was amazing. The journey too! I loved it.

Malik Rahman (10)

Carnegie Primary School, Dunfermline

Emperor

Dear Diary,

I'm running through Tokyo, late for work. I take a shortcut through a construction site but when I get out, I fall into a manhole. I wake with a banging headache. I feel sick. The whole world is spinning. I hear a woman shouting for Akihito. I realise I am Akihito and I have been reincarnated. Akihito is the name of the son of Emperor Snowa!

Cruz McKenzie (10)

Carnegie Primary School, Dunfermline

The Incredible Diary Of Stevie Fleur And Her Dog!

Dear Diary,

You will never believe what happened today! I am writing this on a slate with mud because *I am trapped!* It all started when I was walking Bonnie down the river in the Yorkshire Dales. It's all overgrown and mysterious down there so anything green would go unnoticed. Suddenly, Bonnie stopped sniffing and turned her head. I could hear it too, this quiet twinkling sound. I was terrified! What was it? Then all of a sudden, I saw it, a glowing green portal! I felt nervous but I knew I had to explore. Then I stepped in...

Dottie Bolton (11)

Collingham Lady Elizabeth Hastings CE Aided Primary School, Collingham

The Mysterious Feathers

I woke up to a *bang-whoosh* coming from the stables! Scared, I wondered what had happened. I went to the stables. Cookie, Daisy, Spirit and Shadow were fine, but when I looked at Peggy she wasn't there, only feathers. A whining came from outside, Peggy - but with beautiful silver wings! She cantered then... she was off flying like you've never seen before! Backflips, running on air, everything you could think! She dived down and gracefully landed while putting her wings away and walked back to her stall like nothing had happened.

Skye Mizen (11)

Collingham Lady Elizabeth Hastings CE Aided Primary School, Collingham

The Super Saving Of 9/11

Dear Diary,

You will never believe what happened! Yesterday, I was working on my time machine. *Boom!* Suddenly, I was in 2001, I was so scared. That's when it hit me, I was in New York. Everything seemed normal until... *Crash!* The Twin Towers had been hit. I then glitched back into 2023. I was trying to warn everyone but they wouldn't listen so I went back to 2001 and told everyone not to board the plane. They actually lisented! No one was hurt and now I'm all over the news. Now isn't that crazy! Wow!

Delilah Potter (10)

Collingham Lady Elizabeth Hastings CE Aided Primary School, Collingham

The Diary Of Bethany Bucket: The Day I Went Through A Black Hole

You will never believe what happened yesterday! Being strapped into a massive roller coaster, I was super nervous but my mum comforted me. As we shot up into the sky, something strange appeared - a black dot slowly growing and growing until... *Crash!* I was tumbling through the sky. My head bumped into something that looked like a white tree. Confused as to what had happened, I started to slowly get up, and I saw it. An elf! At least that's what I thought it was. Suddenly, a shiver went down my spine. I was at the North Pole.

Millie Murgatroyd (10)

Collingham Lady Elizabeth Hastings CE Aided Primary School, Collingham

The Crazy Diary Of Emelia Stocken

You will not believe what happened! My holiday visit took a drastic turn. I got off the plane, two bodyguards escorting me to a secret organisation. I was absolutely terrified. Men were dressed in black suits, staring me down, holding guns. A woman shouted to go with her. A man explained I was going to kill someone. Kill someone! The nerves were building up. A black suit was laid out with a gun. The helicopter travelled across to Trafalgar Square. I pulled the trigger and I just missed. I pulled it again and it hit. We had done it! Yes!

Sophie Townley (11)

Collingham Lady Elizabeth Hastings CE Aided Primary School, Collingham

The Diary Of A Perfectly Normal Boy

Dear Diary,

You'll never believe what happened today when I went to walk my dog. If you told me this morning when I woke up that I'd be a millionaire by the end of the day, I would have erupted into laughter, yet it happened anyway. Whilst walking down the street, I spotted £2 lodged underneath a grate. I approached it, wondering what I would do with it. The next thing I knew, I was walking into a shop and buying a lottery ticket with my dad. Which is why I'm writing this from the comfort of my new mansion.

Nell Pickersgill (10)

Collingham Lady Elizabeth Hastings CE Aided Primary School, Collingham

I'm A Suffragette!

You'll never believe what happened today! At the library, I found a book about the suffragettes. I found a page on the Pankhurst family tree. Guess what? My name was there! Me! Beatrice Pankhurst! Suddenly, I was sucked into a vortex of ticking clocks and I landed on the floor outside the library. I'm so lucky that I still had my diary in my bag! A lady was staring, standing near the door to a factory. She asked what happened, who I was and if I wanted her to help me get back home. She was the amazing Sylvia Pankhurst!

Sophie Bailey (10)

Collingham Lady Elizabeth Hastings CE Aided Primary School, Collingham

Where Did My Parents Go?

While in class, my headteacher asked to borrow me. I was scared. She wrapped her arm around me and told me my parents had tragically died; she drove me home and told me my sister would be there soon. Sitting on my steps, I heard the echo of the door shut. I sank to the floor and cried until I couldn't breathe. I dragged myself to the TV, flipped on the news; there was nothing about the plane crash my headteacher had told me about. I looked everywhere, nothing. I ran to the police station, then it all went black...

Eidy Johnson (10)
Collingham Lady Elizabeth Hastings CE Aided Primary School, Collingham

Would I Ever Be Able To Go To The Opportunity Of A Lifetime?

You will never guess what happened. When I woke up, I checked my phone. Not knowing who the email was from, I clicked it open and realised it was from the amazing pro dancer Ava Hill (from the Royal Ballet) saying 'We would love you to be the lead ballerina'. Crying, I wondered how I would get there. I live in Newcastle whereas the Royal Ballet is in Manchester. Somehow, I would have to try and get there (my dad is working in Sweden and my mum is working in the hospital). Would I ever be able to go?

Sophie Fraser (11)

Collingham Lady Elizabeth Hastings CE Aided Primary School, Collingham

I Woke Up On The Titanic!

I had the strangest day yesterday. I woke up in 1912 on the Titanic while a sea monster was attacking the ship. So I rushed inside. I could hear screaming coming from all directions. The shaking stopped so I went to find the cabin. I saw the captain curled up in the corner of the room. I said, "Drive the boat, or I will." So the captain put his brave face on and started the engine. I stood up and fell. I hit the floor hard.

I woke up. "Maybe it was a dream," I whispered to myself.

Austin Reeve (10)

Collingham Lady Elizabeth Hastings CE Aided Primary School, Collingham

Where Is Rosie?

Today in class, I was waiting for Rosie, but she didn't arrive. I was starting to get worried. When school ended, I went to her house to see if she was alright. Her parents explained to me that she had passed away. My whole world collapsed, it took me a minute to realise that this was reality. She's gone. I wanted to know more. I went back to her house to investigate. I searched around. I found a secret door and heard a rumble. I opened the door and there she was, cold, shivering and all alone...

Annie Penrose (11)

Collingham Lady Elizabeth Hastings CE Aided Primary School, Collingham

How My World Went Backwards

You'll never guess what happened today. Recently, I've noticed that my reflection has been fading and today I found that it was gone! I touched my mirror and I fell right through! I stood up in the exact same room. There was a knock on the door. I went to open it but ran into my bed. What? I opened my door to see a goblin on the floor. I bent down to pick it up but it leapt up onto my face! I stumbled backwards, back through my mirror. Little did I know, this goblin held an infectious disease...

William Driver (11)

Collingham Lady Elizabeth Hastings CE Aided Primary School, Collingham

Time Travel Or Dream?

You will never believe this, I woke up as a flight attendant on 9/11. I was confused. I went to the cockpit to see a pilot unconscious. I sprinted to first class to grab a chair. I sprinted towards the cockpit and I put on an intrepid face. I smashed the door down and smashed it onto the terrorist's head with blood gushing everywhere and skulls grinding onto jaws. I safely hijacked the plane to a safe landing. Then the emotions were rushing through my head like a river.
Then I woke up as me.

Teddy Smitherman (11)

Collingham Lady Elizabeth Hastings CE Aided Primary School, Collingham

My Mum - The Hero

You will never guess what happened today! I woke up and I was in the past. I was confused but this man was next to me. So he must have been my dad. He said Mum was out and he was going to get a whip. I was confused but I wanted to go and find Mum to tell her. Found her! She was at a suffragette meeting. But I went to go and tell her and this policeman started fighting her. Mum was screaming and I was too. The policeman grabbed her. She was gone. My heart had disappeared...

Lauren Jayne McAllister (11)
Collingham Lady Elizabeth Hastings CE Aided Primary School, Collingham

When I Met June

Dear Diary,

Yesterday, when walking through a forest, I heard a half-jaguar, half-human. I was astonished, people were flying through the sky. It introduced itself as June. I asked her if I could come here every day. However, she said no because her head teacher would be very angry. If she found out, she would make her into a cuddly toy until the end of the day. I agreed because I cared for June. We had the most magical day and June was even allowed over for Sunday dinner which is my favourite. I can't wait to see June again.

M G (11)
Elmwood School, Rushall

Rebecca And Pomeranian Tales

Today I started looking at Pomeranians and wishing I had one. I asked my parents for one and they said when I'm twelve. Right now, I'm currently eleven so that's a year to wait. But I suppose I can wait because it's my dream dog. When I was hungry, I asked my brother what he wanted. The same as me; chicken nuggets and fries. So that's what we had.

I looked on YouTube about how to take care of a Pomeranian. I'll make a presentation about why I need one and show them why I am responsible to own one.

Rebecca Spendlove (11)

Elmwood School, Rushall

The Day I Turned My Teacher Into A Gorilla

Dear Diary,

Today was a crazy day. I turned my teacher into a gorilla! I don't know how but I did! Here's how I did it, I got a 'magic wand' for my 8th birthday. I'm now 11. I decided to take it to school and try and use it. Why? I don't know. I didn't think it would work! It came to English class so I wished, "Please turn into a gorilla, please." And it worked! At the end of the day, I saw that the teacher couldn't get in his car! So that was my day. Bye!

Josie Evans (11)
Elmwood School, Rushall

Creating My Magical Potion

Dear Diary,

Today I made a magical potion. I was at school in my science lesson and the teacher walked out to go to the toilet. When he walked out, I grabbed some liquids from the cupboard he had left open. I quickly tipped them all into a mixing pot and gave it a shake. All of a sudden... *Boom!* The lights went out and the room filled with sweet-smelling smoke. As the lights came on, I was now not surrounded by children but by googly-eyed aliens. I had made a child-changing alien potion.

Charlie Smyth (11)
Elmwood School, Rushall

The Pupil Who Learned To Fly

Dear Diary,

Today was the most magical day of my life. It's not something I can tell anyone about so it needs to stay a secret. My day started normally by going to school but at lunchtime, I felt a funny feeling inside. I was thinking happy thoughts when my feet started to lift off the ground. I was scared at first but as I hovered, I began to feel calm. The happier the thoughts I felt, the higher I soared. I was actually flying! Tomorrow, I am going to try again and see how high I can go!

Jon Jones (11)
Elmwood School, Rushall

Shooting In Oxford

It was dark when I woke. It was an early start. We climbed into the pick-up for Oxford. It would take about two and a half hours. We got to Oxford and Bowl brought the guns. He handed me one. Bowl loaded it with bullets and we began shooting pigeons. Shayla collected the dead pigeons from the ground because we hadn't got a dog. I shot and clipped its wing. I didn't kill it so it flew away. I did manage to get the next one. We do this to help the farmer. It saves his crops from being eaten.

R-Jay Manby (11)
Elmwood School, Rushall

The Jungle

Dear Diary,

Yesterday it was terrible. As I got on the plane to go to Spain, it crashed. Then as the plane crashed, the plane's pilot said, "This is it, goodbye!" And then *boom!* The plane crashed as we fell we hit the ground and I thought, *did all of us survive? Is the plane okay? Is the plane pilot okay? Will we all make it out alive or will we die?* But then, we saw a tree fall down and then heard a scream. Then we saw a huge spider, the size of a tree...

Riley Cabrera (12)
Elmwood School, Rushall

The Best Day Ever

Today was the best day ever because I scored a hat-trick. One of the goals was an overhead kick and a rabona and a top left and Gareth Bale got me 'Man of the Match' because I scored. I was playing a football match and my team won the match. We played the match at my school. I am feeling very proud because we won and I can't wait for the next match. I can't wait for my next match because I am playing up front and want to score more goals to be like Ronaldo and play football.

Junior Stansbie (11)
Elmwood School, Rushall

My Scary Nightmare

Dear Diary,

I had the scariest nightmare ever. It was a lovely sunny day at the beach until I heard a massive bang and I looked at the sea. I could see lots of pirate signs anchoring at port. Pirates were moving towards the bay. I took action with my net gun I was tackled by a pirate and taken to their ship. Spider-Man came to the rescue to take back his web gun I had stolen. We then became sidekicks and fought all of them. Then it went black. I woke up from the nightmare, scared.

Harry-Lee (11)

Elmwood School, Rushall

The Mass Destruction Of Brexit

Dear Diary,
Today, I landed on a new planet. My spaceship computer told me it was called Earth. As I stepped off the spaceship, I saw humans. They looked horrified and ran off. I chased after them and ate them one by one. It was fun for a while. Then I got bored and flew to a place called France and hunted more humans. I then flew to the big tower that they have, the Eiffel Tower, and blew it up. They screamed loudly in fear and I laughed at them as they died and I flew away.

Rhys Sheamar (11)
Elmwood School, Rushall

The Day I Travelled Back In Time

As I opened the door, I was transported back in time. I could see Grandad but he was much younger than I remembered him. His hair was no longer white but long and dark. But there was no mistaking that wonderful smile and laugh. We chatted but he was obviously unaware of who I was due to not even being born yet. He told me all about his time in the war and how he met my nan. It was so wonderful but I needed to get back home as my mom was cooking lasagne. I loved this day.

Simon Smith (11)
Elmwood School, Rushall

Unplant Panic

Something truly strange has happened. My aunt, who's also named Daffodil, came over. Mum was completely enraged. She tried to hide it, but we all knew that she despised 'The Botanist'. The Botanist, however, seemed to just be focused on... me.

"Daffy, dear," she cooed simperingly, "come help me with something."

Mum was an irate bull. Aunt Daff held out some seeds. Were they from her job in Argentina? Noo... They were daffodils! *Whoosh!* Suddenly, daffodils were growing on my hands! Unbelievable! I stared in awe. Curious, delighted. This was going to change my life! But... what about my mum?

Arike Shokanmbi (11)

Northlands Primary School And Nursery, Pitsea

The Life Of A Pencil (A Child's Entertainment)

In Shara's room, pencils came to life. Whatever they drew came to life as well. One day, they drew a broken heart. Then everyone argued (why did they do this?). The next day, they drew fire!

"Argh! Everyone's in danger."

"Don't fear, Glitter is here." Glitter is the super pencil. "I'm here to help. You grab the water bucket!"

"Thanks."

She started putting it out. People were hiding in a bunker. After, Glitter shouted, "Come out!" People rushed to their loved ones. The town was sad, their homes were gone! They gathered and worked as a team to fix this.

Amelia Vernazza (11)

Northlands Primary School And Nursery, Pitsea

The Wysteria Hidden Within Me

Dear Diary,

Everyone has a wysteria (a power common rare ultra legendary). Everywhere I go, it never stops. "Mum! Look at this. Look at what I can do!"

I'm just fed up. Each human has a power, but you have to find them across the world. Dad says I already have a hidden power but I don't believe him, nor know what he's talking about. Soon after, I ran away from home, desiring to find my wysteria. Police looking for me, scattered everywhere. I'm on the run, hopelessly. What's next? Do I succeed or not?

Yours sincerely Diary,

Hikimaru Yeager.

Daniel Arthur (11)

Northlands Primary School And Nursery, Pitsea

The Game

Yesterday was the worst. Here's what happened. It was cold, dark and scary when I was taken to a mysterious dark, red room with nine other frightened people shivering like jelly. I was questioning why I was here. Someone came out (host) and said, "The game has begun." Everyone screamed as the room became pitch-black... Someone was walking around singing. When I turned back and forth, I heard a small splat. I screamed as loud as 60 leaf blowers being used at once. The host said, "The killer has struck!" Will I be back or dead or terrified forever?

Edwardine Nimoh-Ababio (11)
Northlands Primary School And Nursery, Pitsea

The Incredible Diary Of Ash May

Dear Diary,

There's a war happening about whether I'm Lila Hollywood or Ash May, but what they don't know is that I suffer from an identification disorder, meaning those two people are my different personalities.

My mother hates serial killers, but I started falling in love with murder. At first, I deeply regretted killing people but now it's a part of my life and I can't take it away from myself. Ash May is my serial killer personality.

In an hour, I need to go to a concert in Japan but I'm afraid the people outside are gonna see me.

Sophie Tressider (10)

Northlands Primary School And Nursery, Pitsea

Life

My name is Terrence Tunner. I love football and basketball. My favourite team is Manchester United. I can kick high and shoot in ginormous hoops. I love pizza and chicken. I like learning about Egypt. I have a little brother called Arthur and he likes Spider-Man and he's in nursery. I collect football cards and Pokémon cards. I have Kylian Mbappé, Cristiano Ronaldo, Son Heung-min and Vinícius Junior. I would love to learn about the Egyptian pharaoh, Khufee. Did you know that Cleopatra married Julius Caesar and Marc Anthony? I'm in year three.

Terrence Turner (7)

Northlands Primary School And Nursery, Pitsea

Gravitational Haze

I was flying through space, sending asteroids off course and helping the thriving Mars become habitable for humans. Zoning out in space is like a sensory deprivation tank in itself. Mining resources on asteroids can be a hassle, especially when you're on a time limit. My sight... it went very blurry and... my body shut down. And then... extreme pain came moving a millimetre... My memory... a haze labyrinth. My lungs were dishevelled and my vision was a complete fog. *Huh,* I thought. People were crying around me and I could hear them for some weird reason...

Olley Ricci (10)
Northlands Primary School And Nursery, Pitsea

The Green Book!

Dear Diary,

Today was as boring as always because I just sat in a dark, wooden, old cupboard with everyone else. I mean, I am a green, mossy colour (everyone's favourite colour in the classroom). But I don't get why no one likes me because I'm about a tree that's getting left behind by people that chop down trees (well the tree is lucky because it doesn't get chopped down, right?) Yesterday, I had the best day of my life because a Reception class came in and read me because they are learning about trees!

Yours sincerely,

Green Book.

Nancy Bleu (10)

Northlands Primary School And Nursery, Pitsea

The Fox Who Went To The Moon

Dear Diary,

Today's been an amazing adventure. I travelled to the moon! I was suited up ready to go. Sorry, I should've introduced myself. My name's Fluffy the Fox, there I was looking at the towering rocket above. I stepped in, 5, 4, 3, 2, 1, blast-off! *Zoom*, I travelled to the moon! *Bang!* I landed and jumped so high, searching for aliens. *Squeak.* There's one! I had fun playing with my alien friend before it was time to go back home. I'm so excited to share this with my fox friends and be the first fox on the moon.

Jessica Perry (9)

Northlands Primary School And Nursery, Pitsea

The Incredible Diary Of Captain America

Dear Diary,

Today, I helped save thousands of people with the Avengers. Sadly, Black Widow and T'Challa died. Hawkeye went back to New York with Spider-Man. While Hulk visited She Hulk in LA, Thor travelled back to Asgard as Loki is no longer a threat.

After the war, I travelled back in time to see Agent Peggy Carter. I gave my shield to Falcon. A good friend Antman (or Scott) left with the Wasp to fight another day. I miss the Avengers. Tony died killing Thanos. He might have been annoying but he was a hero.

Yours sincerely,

Captain America.

Keeon Downes (11)

Northlands Primary School And Nursery, Pitsea

The War Of Good And Evil - Part One

Allan's eyes blinked twice, trying to stay awake, class had been on forever! He picked up his pencil and continued the assignment, while distracted, his bully (Wade) snuck up behind him. Before Wade could touch him, lightning struck them. Their screams boomed through the school. Allan slowly awoke, his hands and arms were stiff. Sitting himself up, he turned his attention to his waist. A blade rested on his side. With full intention, he removed it from its sheathe. The blade shone red and black while his left hand was engulfed in flames. This was not school...

Geremi Rous (11)

Northlands Primary School And Nursery, Pitsea

The Heaven Queen

Dear Diary,

Today was tiring. It was a three realms meeting (Heaven, Hell and Overworld). I was late by a whole ten minutes. I was travelling through portals when I found I was in Aradon and I was Mal! Amelia was Evie. She was confused as well when Ben came up to me. Evie said, "What do we do?" "I don't know," I replied. "Let's try and run out of here so we can figure something out."

Evie then suggested using portals and it worked but I was in a Mal dress. It was really cool in Aradon.

Bye,

Ella.

Ella Tice (10)

Northlands Primary School And Nursery, Pitsea

How I Died Unexpectedly

Dear Diary,

I went exploring in a forest practising my cheer dance but little did I know an alien was lurking in the mysterious forest looking for someone to capture. I had no idea about it.

I heard a clinking noise in the distance. As I got closer towards it I got scared and screamed which notified the alien to chase me and I was not being cautious knowing about it.

Many hours later, the alien captured me and possessed me on a tree. Sadly, I died unexpectedly without anybody knowing.

After a couple of years, I'm still lurking.

Lola-Belle Philip (11)

Northlands Primary School And Nursery, Pitsea

A Great Day

Dear Diary,

Today was a great day as I made a discovery. It started when I was in school and I went down to the science lab. I noticed a glowing portal. I thought, *why is this here?* As I got closer, my hand was starting to disintegrate. After a while, I was transported to another world! I looked around and I saw loads of Pokémon roaming around! I've always wanted to catch a Pokémon. I saw a Scorbunny holding a Pokéball. It wanted me to catch it. I had been researching about Scorbunny. It evolves into a Raboot.

Jessica Broom (9)
Northlands Primary School And Nursery, Pitsea

The Mysterious Egg

Dear Diary,
Today something strange happened to me. I entered a forest and I found an extremely large egg. Curiously, I looked around for its mother but there was nobody to be seen. I took it home.
Once it was all tucked up, it was time for lights out. I tried to sleep. However, my mind kept racing. Then the strangest thing happened. My room was filled with a purple glow and I heard a faint tapping. Nervously, I approached the now glowing egg. I could see a flame poking from a crack. What on Earth was inside?
Yours,
Amelia.

Amelia Lefever (11)

Northlands Primary School And Nursery, Pitsea

Time Travel Everywhere On Earth

Dear Diary,
My name is Kwaku and you don't know what happened. When I was about to go to bed, then a glittering beautiful wishing star drifted past houses. I wished quickly before it could go past me as quick as lightning. I wished for me to look into the precious, good-looking planets to see the aliens or people that live there permanently. I also wished, looking to all of the green, mostly aquamarine sea of Earth, to go back many years before Christ.
When I woke up, everything came true. I was on a shimmering, amazing planet.

Owuraku Asiedu (8)
Northlands Primary School And Nursery, Pitsea

Diary Of A Girl With Wings

Dear Diary,

Today was terrifying! As usual, I went to school and was yet again met by the faces of those who hate me the most. Anyway, skipping to after lunch, I was sitting by my favourite tree, reading a book. Did I mention that I had wings?

I looked up as I heard people screaming. To my surprise, I saw a large rock flying at us - it was a meteor! I rushed forward, lifting my wings. Suddenly, multiple blue lightning bolts struck at it, making the meteor disappear. I stared in disbelief - had I really just saved everyone here?

Zuzanna Adamska (10)

Northlands Primary School And Nursery, Pitsea

The Big Fight

Dear Diary,

Today me and my friend Summer Alexandra Nenorea went outside and then something terrible happened. I (nearly) broke my arm because of my bully Rebecca. She looks nice and caring but she's actually a devil (the news that is about to be said is shocking). I threw a metal bottle at her because she tried hitting Summer so she came to attack me. So she jumped onto me and it broke out into a fight and I won so me and Summer set off for a wonderful adventure to a place called Sydney, Australia.

Bye,

From Frankie.

Raylan Hewlett (11)

Northlands Primary School And Nursery, Pitsea

The Time Before Time

Dear Diary,
Today I was in my garage with my friend Jacob, trying to make a flying model plane with wood, nails and many other materials including chemicals. Little did we know, when Jacob mixed two chemicals, a little dot appeared in mid-air that grew bigger at an alarming rate. It stopped at 6ft long and wide. It was a portal... Me and Jacob looked at each other and he told me to go inside it. Thinking I was dreaming, I stepped inside. All was dark. Nothingness. I think I'm going to call it... 'The Time Before Time'.

Tommy Hayhoe (11)
Northlands Primary School And Nursery, Pitsea

Life In Space... Forever

Dear Diary,

Today is the third of April 2023, three days after the disaster. My oxygen is running low and my food and water aren't much better. I have been sending SOS signals for hours but I'm still waiting on a response from my launch team. If you're reading this (which you're probably not) please tell my mum I'm sorry for running away and I wish I never did. My radar says that I am on course with a meteorite that will rip my spaceship to shreds. I have lost all faith and my escape has been damaged. Goodbye.

Jack Hodges (11)
Northlands Primary School And Nursery, Pitsea

Diary Of The Holiday Disaster

Dear Diary,

After a two-hour journey of traffic, me and my family finally made it to our destination. However, when Dad asked for our tickets and signed in, the worker said she had no idea who we were! Then we realised we were at the wrong destination. Luckily, we were only ten minutes away.

When we finally made it to the right destination, we had to take a lift to the hotel. As me and my family made it, we were devastated! For starters, there was only one bed. However, things turned around when we went to do some swimming.

Chloe Wincott (9)

Northlands Primary School And Nursery, Pitsea

Mrs Bear's Adventure

It's me, Mrs Bear. I am back from a hectic adventure. It all started on a Wednesday. My owner (who is an adorable ten-year-old) grabbed me by the arm and dashed downstairs. We went off on a big bad aeroplane. They are so so scary! As we went to Hawaii, suddenly I heard a big boom! A menacing robot voice stated, "We have crashed and landed in Mexico!" As we cautiously stepped out of the plane, we saw scary people outside in purple clothes and skeleton masks. Are they even humans?
Love Mrs Bear.
See you soon.

Yara Yousf (10)
Northlands Primary School And Nursery, Pitsea

A Day In The Air

Dear Diary,

I had the most petrifying day of my life! It started with a patrol in an F4 Phantom (a multi-role aircraft). A handful of fifth-generation fighters appeared on radar and were all over the place. Soon, they were locking on to friendly aircraft so me and my radar monitor went into a cobra manoeuvre and shot down each and every YOR-31 aircraft until a very disturbing thing happened. Our engine was on fire, causing me and the co-pilot to eject. As soon as we did, we were bombarded with fire until the RAF picked us up.

Ollie White (10)

Northlands Primary School And Nursery, Pitsea

My Sister Shouts At Me

Dear Diary,

One day, I was playing on my iPad when suddenly, it died! I was so sad but then I remembered my older sister (Ellie). That's when I thought I should go and see what she was up to. And that's what I did. So I entered her room and she was on a call with her friend as always. I asked her, "Ellie, what are you doing?"

Then she said, "I'm on a call with my friends."

I said, "Okay."

She asked me to exit her room but I said no. Then she shouted. Mum took her side.

Ellie Sartin (10)
Northlands Primary School And Nursery, Pitsea

The Poor Ruler

Dear Diary,
Today at school, I was trodden on six times before my owner came and got me right before maths. You see, my life is hard. I'm pretty much used for every lesson at school. It is the worst thing you could imagine. I was so excited when I got picked. It turns out there was nothing to be excited about. I have been bent, nearly snapped and dropped. I don't know how I will survive. Four days ago, a child threw me over a fence. They might never find me but at least I'm home.
Yours sincerely,
Ruler.

Lily-Rose Knight (10)
Northlands Primary School And Nursery, Pitsea

Winter Uprising

Dear Diary,

Today I thought to myself, I'm not good enough. I can't stand being a frail, not above-average man. I'm gonna change. I will change and prove I'm the best and cannot be defeated. It has come to my attention I'm not the strongest but I know who is and I'll put all my power into defeating him. He is known as Destroyer but he is Ronan. This man is a monstrous beast and goes to the gym every day. He's even a heavyweight boxing champion meaning I need to be him to beat him, which I will be.

Georgie Bennett (10)

Northlands Primary School And Nursery, Pitsea

Pencil Explaining What He Wants

Dear Diary,
Last Saturday night, at exactly 12am, I was striding through the thorny wood. As soon as I walked in the door of my cottage, I heard a snap. *Bang!* It was an extremely large pencil with a book. I wasn't bothered so I went to bed. Suddenly, I woke up. Then I saw this huge pencil explaining something in the book. It read, 'Please sharpen me. I'm only the height I used to be'. I thought, *well, I don't have a sharpener to fit the pencil in.* So I tried to forget it and went to bed.

Abbie Gregson (10)

Northlands Primary School And Nursery, Pitsea

The Discovery Of The Rarest Dragon Known

Dear Diary,

I am critically surprised by how I found this. But I did and it's a reality. While I was near a lake (sitting on the cliff, peering down upon the lake and waterfall) I felt that I was being watched. I dashed around my back and saw my cruel family, having an angry expression. They tried to push me over. Then I dodged it, making them fall into the burning hot springs (a part of the lake). I looked down mercilessly at the burning, painful shrieks of my now-burned parents. Then, I found the rarest dragon known...

Agata Odinas (11)

Northlands Primary School And Nursery, Pitsea

James The Mightios

Dear Diary,
Today, James created a new idea like every day. He made a pirate with a cat, a man with twenty-one legs and a girl with twenty-nine cats! Then, he made a school in his mind with monsters, pirates, ships on the water and a golden temple. He made a sea monster that eats boats for breakfast, lunch and dinner. Just then, James made a kid with a superpower, a boy who runs into the sea. Then, all of his creations came to life! After that, he said to me, "Save the day," said James, "and end this!"

Lewis Morrell (10)

Northlands Primary School And Nursery, Pitsea

The Zombie-Dinosaur War

Dear Diary,

Today we had a science competition at school. Me and my friends created a time machine. Everybody wanted to try, but before you know it, it was already over. But today it felt like it would never end. Brad the bully and his gang came to try it. They went back to dinosaur times and started a zombie-dinosaur war. They rushed out of the door and roamed our streets. The mayor decided to send our best army fighters. They shot every dinosaur in sight and eventually won the war. Anyway, I got an award.

See you soon.

Logan Gardiner (11)

Northlands Primary School And Nursery, Pitsea

Diary Of An Alien: Everyone Is Different

Dear Diary,

My name is Zog and I am an alien. I currently live on this planet called 'The Moon' but today I am moving house on a new planet called 'Mars'. This also means I have to move schools. On the day I left, I said goodbye, depressed, to my friends and then left in the flying saucer. When I arrived, I got dressed into my uniform and went to my new school. Everyone here was different from me so I quickly got bullied by this guy called River. Then, someone named Cody came to me and changed everything.

Elliot Adom (9)

Northlands Primary School And Nursery, Pitsea

Paula The Polar Bear

Dear Diary,

My name is Paula the polar bear. I have been having to starve for a while since there's not enough food for me and my family but every day I go out for hours and I find barely anything. Today, I have been looking for more than three hours and I didn't find anything. I don't want me and my family to go hungry since it's been almost three days since I have eaten. My little sister died yesterday from starvation. Anyway, I have to look again. Just in case.

Yours sincerely,

Polar Paula.

Julia Sikora (11)

Northlands Primary School And Nursery, Pitsea

The Exhausting Year Of Archie The Ant

Dear Diary,

My name is Archie the Ant. I'm here to tell you how stressful my days are from getting picked up and trodden on. Nearly every single day, I always have a dark shadow over me which is the size of a shoe so that's how I know to always stay underground and always run fast. Another thing that I hate is whenever I'm on a leaf, people choose to pick them and give them to other people so I technically travel around the world. When you kids are older, I hope you learn from this.

From,

Archie.

Tegan Down (11)

Northlands Primary School And Nursery, Pitsea

The Champions League Final

Dear Diary,

Today might be a hard day. I have been chosen to be the ball that is going to be used in the Champions League final. Firstly, I was carried onto the pitch by the referee and then placed on the kick-off spot which is at halfway. Then, I watched the captains do the coin toss to see who gets kick-off. Arsenal got the kick-off and there we went, I was kicked. It was the ninety-fifth minute and there was only one minute and then Arsenal scored. The score was now 2-1 to Arsenal. Bakayo Saka scored the winner.

Kai Harrison (10)

Northlands Primary School And Nursery, Pitsea

The Proposal Disaster

Zendaya woke up, not knowing she would soon be Zendaya Holland. She set out to Time Square just as Tom Holland had asked her. As she saw him, she ran and hugged while smiling. As she turned around, Tom got on one knee and asked her to marry him. Zendaya screamed and jumped into the air. Then... *Boom!* She fell unconscious as she fainted. After six hours, she awoke. Tom rushed her to the hospital. She stayed for a few days. Then, when Tom took her home, they both sat on the couch, put on a film and fell asleep.

Siena Wallace

Northlands Primary School And Nursery, Pitsea

The Humpless Camel

One day, King Tut was riding his camel in the golden, sandy desert when he stopped in shock. He saw a lonely humpless camel. The camel was sad. King Tut loved animals and camels were his favourite. He told his servant to bring the camel back to the pyramid palace. Over the next few weeks, King Tut spent many hours stroking, feeding and talking to the camel. He even made him a hump which made the camel happy. King Tut trusted the camel and found him a job for life, storing all his jewels and treasures in his fake hump.

Halle Adams (8)

Northlands Primary School And Nursery, Pitsea

The Great Escape Of Pedro The Pencil

Dear Diary,

My name is Pedro the Pencil and I have been mistreated by the malicious humans! A little boy grabbed me and started scraping my nose on a piece of paper; I was in tears. Ever since that day, my nose has shortened. The next day, I was stomped on by another boy but this time I was mad so I tried to roll out of the class and I actually escaped! Finally, I was free from the disastrous children and now I can live without my nose being scraped and my body being stomped on.

Yours sincerely,

Pedro.

Yanel Senour (11)

Northlands Primary School And Nursery, Pitsea

The Good Day Of An English Book

Dear Diary,

Today was so good. It has been a fun day at school for the children so nobody used me today. Nobody drew or wrote or scribbled in me all day. Today was about having time to myself so I slept all day and dreamed about it being a lovely day with me sunbathing at the hot beach and swimming in the sea. I was drinking a lovely tropical cocktail with lemon. It was so nice til I got woken up by someone offering me some lemonade. I kindly accepted it. It was so yummy.

Yours sincerely,

English Book.

Layla Atherton (11)

Northlands Primary School And Nursery, Pitsea

The Calm Alien

Dear Diary,

I have crashed on Earth due to a power outage. So until I have all the bars, I'm living in the basement of a family house. From time to time, I hypnotise the owners into being my servants. You know, to bring me snacks and build machines. I mean who knew the human body could do so much? But then again, they're lacking in limbs and attachments. Like who still has two arm and legs anymore? It's a tad outdated. That was my day so far.

Xyphare, or alien as everyone calls me on Earth. Bye.

George Costen (11)
Northlands Primary School And Nursery, Pitsea

How I Won A War (A Rock)

Dear Diary,

Today I was selected by a special agent to go to war. Feeling nervous, I was transported to training as sweat rolled down the side of my red cheek. I was designed to shoot out guns, and knives, to give the enemies a fatal blow. Standing as stiff as a soldier, the carpet of green surrounded everyone as we went to war. Excited to win, I shot out knives and killed many rivals. Bullets were like lightning striking a building. We won the war! Hope to speak to you soon. Laters, from a super fantastic Rock.

Samuel Olatunji (10)

Northlands Primary School And Nursery, Pitsea

The Tail Story

Dear Diary,
Today I have been pooped on and scratched. I have been wagging for nearly the whole day. Then, I was sad. After that, my owner got adopted by someone pretty (everyone is pretty). Now, I am taken care of and have been cleaned every day. I love my new life because it's... awesome! I don't get pooped on now and I'm very thankful for this because I don't get dirty anymore (for long). This new life is the best! And the fact that I have a bath every day is awesome! It's fun to be here!

Alessia Garril (10)

Northlands Primary School And Nursery, Pitsea

The Great Adventure

Dear Diary,

Today was very intriguing as my mother found the key to the basement door. To my surprise, I saw the most beautiful doorway I had ever seen. As I am the most nosy and curious person, I went through. My mind was blown, as through this door I saw a turquoise, blue waterfall overhanging a cliff. On top of this cliff lay a gorgeous castle. I ran up the hill, trying to imagine what could be inside. Surprisingly, it was a giant throne, perfectly placed in the middle of the room. That was the best day for me.

Camelia Aioanei (11)

Northlands Primary School And Nursery, Pitsea

The GOAT Of Football Is Here

Dear Diary,
I am a footballer and I love playing football. I train every day to become the GOAT of football and I am getting there. My name is Lionel Messi and my result of playing is getting better and better. That means I am getting better and better after each of the games. Over a hundred, a thousand, a million, maybe even a billion fans love my style of playing. After one year, I finally achieved my goal as the GOAT of football. Basically, all the fans in the world love me and I am grateful for that.

Jayden Andah (10)
Northlands Primary School And Nursery, Pitsea

Dear Diary

Dear Diary,

I was excited when I was in cross-country. Year two arrived. As year two were done, I felt in happiness once I was doing laps. In a flash, I was speedier than everybody else. A second later, I was growing huge, muscular legs with vivid colourful spots on me. As I was growing those humongous legs, I was growing phosphorescent incandescent claws. I am perplexed by what is going on. My skin was becoming variegated. I don't know what's happening now. I can metamorphose when I'm hysterical!

Gabriel Sava (8)
Northlands Primary School And Nursery, Pitsea

The Greatest Day

Dear Diary,

One sunny morning, I was playing hide-and-seek with my sister when suddenly a golden key caught my eye. It was as bright as a diamond. I called my sister to come here and explore the golden key. Once I touched the key, in a blink of an eye, we were in Paris. There were croissants and baguettes everywhere. Once we had finished exploring, we ran to the Eiffel Tower and as soon as we got there it collapsed. Luckily, I had the golden key. Our great but dangerous experience was over and it was fun.

Anthony Atiase (7)

Northlands Primary School And Nursery, Pitsea

The Mystery Cookie

Dear Diary,

It was baking today. We were making cookies. Add flour, sugar and eggs. You know that stuff. Now, let's put them in the oven. It's ready now. Let it cool down and eat it. It was nearly bedtime so I only had one. Goodnight.

The next morning, I was in Brazil. But how did I get here? I wanted to go home. *Knock. Knock.* I wondered who was there. It was Mum. What was she doing here? I wondered, did she know I was here? I bet it was the mystery cookie. Oh oh. But where was Dad?

Ruby Nichols (10)

Northlands Primary School And Nursery, Pitsea

The Blue Boy

Dear Diary,

I woke up in the middle of the night and suddenly I realised I was blue! I rapidly ran downstairs to tell my mum about this tragic event but she wasn't anywhere to be found. Suddenly. I heard an eerie noise in the attic. Remembering what my mum said, I stayed put. But I was tempted too, so I slowly crawled to the attic. Slowly and steadily, I crawled down the stairs to the wooden attic door, pulling my hand on the metal door knob and opened it. Mysteriously, there were gallons of paint...

David Radulescu (10)

Northlands Primary School And Nursery, Pitsea

My Disaster Day Of Being A Hairbrush

Today was a really hectic day for me. Firstly, my owner brushed their hair and didn't even bother cleaning me up. I have hair stuck in me! Then, she took me to school in her bag, it was so dark and creepy! Also, her school books kept hitting me, I have back pain now! After, I accidentally fell out of the owner's bag and was stuck on the floor for like two hours! Until people were kicking me about everywhere. I ended up by a weird, random stranger picking me up and they were taking me to their home...

Zunaira Chowdhury (10)
Northlands Primary School And Nursery, Pitsea

Transportation Into FIFA

Dear Diary,
A boy called Jack, me, had a football match. We came home. Then I went outside. Then I fell into a sewer and got transported to FIFA 23. I chose to go into the ultimate team. Then I played a game against West Ham. Then I scored three goals out of ten and we won. Then we got sucked out of the game. Then my mum said, "Where have you been? We have been looking for you."
"I was somewhere fun."
Then we went to the base jump for my birthday and I invited my friends.

Jack Carter (9)
Northlands Primary School And Nursery, Pitsea

Uh-Oh! Hydra!

Dear Diary,

Yesterday was my birthday. I was happy. But a Hydra fell to Earth! Then I only had a pen for a present. After I clicked the button what felt like a million times it turned into a sword. So I decided to gather supplies and go to kill the Hydra.

Little did we know, Hulk booted a metal football from a different universe to help us defeat him. As the football came racing towards Earth, luckily it landed on the Hydra's spine, shattering it into a million pieces, killing it instantly.

Zachary Hayward (9)

Northlands Primary School And Nursery, Pitsea

The Diary Of A Ladybug

Dear Diary,

Today was a crazy day of saving Paris. Me and Cat Noir had to rescue one of my friends, Alya, from an Akuma. I didn't want to hurt her but I have to hurt her and break her phone to get the Akuma out. It scared me. I thought she was going to get mad but since she was akumatised, she didn't. After, me and cat, Noir went home and Alya phoned me talking about it and asked what she did when she was akumatised. I just said, "I was too scared to look and hid."

Marinette.

Alaina O'Sullivan (11)

Northlands Primary School And Nursery, Pitsea

Superheros Save The Day

One ordinary day, a group of boys robbed the bank. When the police came, they ran and ran. They kept running until the police found them. The police were tired. They had a little rest. When they woke up, the police stepped into a mouse trap. Their legs got stuck. The boys set a trap. The policemen had a painful time getting the trap off. The group of boys managed to run away. When the police found them, the police arrested them. After they were released, they had learned their lesson and became police.

Qanita Owolabi (7)

Northlands Primary School And Nursery, Pitsea

The Lonely Boy

Dear Diary,
I have had the most exhausting day ever. Raylan
(my best friend) didn't finish his homework so I was
all alone at break time! He even came out and
ignored me. So you won't be surprised by what I
say next. He hung out with my class bully
(Rebecca). She always kicks me in the leg and eats
my lunch. She even told me that she wanted to
fight and I had to eat lunch indoors! Raylan has a
girlfriend called Frankie. She also hates me: I
always hang out with him every day.
Jacob.

Summer Nenada (10)
Northlands Primary School And Nursery, Pitsea

A Day In The Life Of Red The Ruler

Hi. My name is Red the Ruler and I have been tortured today! A little boy grabbed Pedro the Pencil and scraped my head. I could tell the pencil was upset too because it was in tears! The rubber, the spare ruler, the pen, the whiteboard and the pen lid watched in shock. The kid smiled happily since he finished his weird project about a family tree. Suddenly, he knocked me off of the table! A little girl came and trod on me! I almost snapped in two! Thank God the kids had to go home. I can recover now.

Jayden Hall (10)
Northlands Primary School And Nursery, Pitsea

The Mystery Of The Mischievous Maths Class

Dear Diary,
Today was the best day ever! As I reluctantly wandered to school, on the bumpy rough pavement and hopped onto the bus, I met up with my friend Abbie and we strolled into maths class. During maths, we noticed a strange door in the corner of the room, with a tiny chip out the top of it, like a miniature mouse had a nibble from it. At the end of class, we heard a banging sound coming from the door. So rapidly, we sped over to it and opened the door, but there it was... A black shadow.

Millie Tomlin (11)

Northlands Primary School And Nursery, Pitsea

Lonely Knife

Dear Diary,

It is me, knife. My owner threw me in the corner and brought a new cooking knife. I'm so upset but I need a plan to get rid of that knife. I've tried throwing it in the bin but the owner got it out of the bin and cleaned it. I've tried breaking it but it was the new unbreakable knife. It can't break. I've tried hiding it in my new corner. She couldn't find it but I thought she wanted to use me but she found it. I felt so so sad. Why wouldn't she use me?

Khloe McKay (10)
Northlands Primary School And Nursery, Pitsea

The Day In The Life Of A Football

Dear Diary,

Today I was in a football match and I was tired of being kicked by people. I've dreamed of doing to the World Cup Final stadium but I'm here in a normal stadium. I feel tired of getting kicked by football players who kick me softly and hard.

I get sent to the World Cup quarter-finals, semi-finals and final. I'm so happy I finally achieved my football goal. Now I get my vacation and live a happy life after I incredibly scored goals in the World Cup final in Qatar.

Mohab Abdalla (10)

Northlands Primary School And Nursery, Pitsea

The Game

Dear Diary,

Today has been an amazing day. When I was gaming, I accidentally spilled water over my keyboard. It was fine because I was getting a new one. But when I got back from getting a towel, my computer was going mental! As soon as I got close, I had been sucked into the game 'Piggy'... I know the maps but it was hard. I only had ten minutes and I only had the white key left. I ran with the key as the pig chased me. I unlocked the front door. I teleported home. Was it over?

Katie Sweeney (10)

Northlands Primary School And Nursery, Pitsea

The Fire Within

Dear Diary,
Today was amazing. Truly amazing. I was at school playing with my friends when a cloud of dust charged towards me. Then, a shot of pain spread around in my veins. I was engulfed in fire. I saw my body change before my eyes. I was now a werewolf. Then, a ball of fire shot out of my mouth. I wasn't a werewolf, I was a hellhound. I immediately knew what I had to do. It was time for me to go to a school for creatures like me, a school for monsters. Monster High, here I come.

Nathaniel Hayward (11)

Northlands Primary School And Nursery, Pitsea

The Mysterious Footballer

Dear Diary,

Today I woke up in Manchester very excited to go to the greatest football game ever. However, when I got to the stadium I passed the security and there was the greatest football player, KDB, warming up, getting ready to play top-of-the-league Arsenal. As City are still in the FA Cup final we are most likely to win the FA Cup against 4th-in-the-league Man U. As the match carried on KDB scored a beauty of a goal. 1-0 City. We needed one more goal to be top of the league.

Riley Bryant (9)
Northlands Primary School And Nursery, Pitsea

Under The Sea

Dear Diary,
Today, I have had a wonderful adventure under the crystal-blue sea. It all started when I was in the middle of the sea on a boat. Suddenly, something astonishing happened. Everything stopped in my sight, apart from me and the ocean. Then, I got sucked into the ocean. I felt delighted at what had happened as if I was in a dream. Under the sea, I got to watch all of the sea creatures swimming around. I also saw the enormous blue whale that was singing with its peaceful voice.

Ana Serbu (9)
Northlands Primary School And Nursery, Pitsea

A Dragon's Diary

Dear Diary,

Today I have lost many of my once-loved family at the Shadow Realm. First, before it was invaded and renamed 'The Forgotten Realm' to be exact, I'm happy I was taken out with the rest since we haven't seen daylight for almost a decade. Although my job as a warrior is to protect my realm... but oh well. I tried to warn them but as usual, nobody even listened to a word that I said after I overheard a conversation between the Fire Realm and the Water Realm.

Annabelle Wood (9)

Northlands Primary School And Nursery, Pitsea

Pixelated!

Dear Diary,

Today was unusual because as soon as I woke up, a strange portal appeared in front of me. I decided to go in... After I stepped through the portal, it immediately shut. But as I turned around, I suddenly realised that I was in a video game! I was excited because I have always wanted to be inside a video game but I soon became nervous because I only had five lives. Before I knew it, I only had one life left! I knew I had to focus so I did and I completed the entire game.

Jake Oliver (10)

Northlands Primary School And Nursery, Pitsea

The Diary Of Violet Baudelaire

Today, I had an extremely different day. First, me, Klaus and Sunny are officially orphans! Our parents died in our house fire and all we did was play on the beach! Mr Poe (our carer) took us to his home to sleep for the night. The next day, we were sent to our closest living relative, Count Olaf. When we got there, he had a dark house. He showed us his theatre group and they were quite weird as well. He showed us our room and it was just a bed and a hammock. There is a lot more coming!

Betsy Gordon (10)
Northlands Primary School And Nursery, Pitsea

Leaving The Moon

Dear Diary,

Today was a terrible day as I left my planet, (the moon) to know what is like. I felt really anxious when I arrived. Then with my shape-shifting power, I turned into a human but I still barely had any oxygen.

After sixteen years, I left to go back to my own kind, however, when I arrived, everyone disappeared. But they surprised me and they all jumped out from the rocks.

"Wow! That was a lot of fun!" my mom shouted.

"See you tomorrow! Bye!"

Rhayan Parker (10)

Northlands Primary School And Nursery, Pitsea

The Mysterious Box

Dear Diary,
Today I was coming home from shopping with my family. My mum and older sister didn't realise anything but I did... When we got out of the car, I spotted a mysterious box lying on the floor which said 'Open Me'. Out of curiosity, I picked up the box and hid it in my jacket to sneak it upstairs and find out what was inside the odd-looking box. I managed to take it upstairs without getting caught but when I was about to look, my mum called me down for dinner.

Kacey Foster (10)

Northlands Primary School And Nursery, Pitsea

Puss In Boots

Dear Diary,
I just had a fight with Death. It was quite tiring but he gave up trying to kill me once and for all because I had one life left. We fought on a giant crystal star with fire around us and they were a pinkish colour. I am really livid now after that fight with Death. My friends were watching from behind the flames. They are called Kitty Soft Paws and Barito. I am off to see my old friends on Far Far Away island. They are Shrek and Donkey and they live in a huge castle.

Sophie Waldron Brown (10)
Northlands Primary School And Nursery, Pitsea

The Diary Of The Dark Demon

Dear Diary,

Today I'm going to tell you how I became the dark demon. All demons get their magic at the age of sixteen. And that year, all sixteen-year-olds would perform a sacrificial ritual in order to get their powers. You can use water, flowers and dirt to do it. Though, mine was different. They tried all of them and none worked. They used the final option, fire. I was nervous though. It worked and I had become the queen of all of the demons because of how powerful I was.

Amber Merchant (10)

Northlands Primary School And Nursery, Pitsea

I'm The Luckiest Girl In The World!

Dear Diary,
The day I was born, my parents adored me. From buying me expensive presents, to almost buying me a full-on mansion. But luckily, I stopped them. We used to live in Pennsylvania and my mum worked as an accountant and Dad was the CEO of a clothing line. Then we had a big enough amount of money to have a weekend in New York. So as soon as we booked each of us a ticket, we packed our bags and headed to the airport with my dad's old rusty, crusty, musty, rusted truck!

Antonia Atiase (7)
Northlands Primary School And Nursery, Pitsea

An Exciting Adventure

First, I woke up. I heard something so weird so I went to check it out. A blue, unknown portal had appeared! I was puzzled so I went inside. But I was stuck! I felt crammed and uncomfortable but then a black and white cat came out to help me. I escaped and then I explored. I found colourful mushrooms and weird trees but also a white cat. It was on a branch, but I ignored it. Then, I fell into a hole, but then... I woke up. I got my breakfast and tried to hunt down Jerry. So weird...

Anya Muthuthamby (11)

Northlands Primary School And Nursery, Pitsea

The Fairy

Dear Diary,
Today I'm going on an adventure with my friend. I feel so happy that my BFF is coming with me. We're going to have so much fun. My day is going so well. I see fifty baby foxes. I love animals so much. I wish I was one. I love going on adventures so much. I'm going on adventures with my mum, my dad and my friends. I'm going to the forest so I can see a reindeer and a cat. I can even see some big foxes. I'm so excited to get a dog for my birthday.

Ruby Pammen (9)
Northlands Primary School And Nursery, Pitsea

Time Travel

Dear Diary,

Today I was in the woods and saw a box that read, 'Time Travel' so I went inside and pressed a couple of buttons and opened the door. Then, I went inside and found it worked. So then I had a little wander around and I went back to where I first teleported to see if I could find a way back. Then I found a button so I pressed it and I found myself back in the year dated 2023. Then I told everyone what had happened but they didn't believe me. But Mum did.

Elle-Jade Anderson (10)

Northlands Primary School And Nursery, Pitsea

A Day Of A Life As A Pen

Dear Diary,
Today was an exhausting day because I am a pen. To start the day, I did some writing and then someone threw me across the classroom. It kinda hurt but I was fine. After that happened, I got put in a drawer. A while later, a girl picked me up, started carrying me and then she was colouring with me. But she didn't put my lid on me so I had to try it myself. So then I eventually did it! I was really tired so I waited for all of the children to go home and rested.

Gracie Oliver (9)

Northlands Primary School And Nursery, Pitsea

A Student Who Entered A Video Game

Dear Diary,

Today I fought a Hydra after I got sucked into a game. Let me tell you how it happened. I just got home after school so I changed and ate dinner. After that, I went to play on my game. A huge emerald-green glow appeared around my living room. I started to fade into the game... I asked myself, "How did I end up here?" After a while, a game tutorial popped up and it explained I had to slay a hydra to beat the game. "How is that even possible?"

Meshach Ngoma Minzako (9)

Northlands Primary School And Nursery, Pitsea

The Tiger

Dear Diary,
It was a cold gloomy night when an orange and black tiger went into a little town called Chicken Wood. It is a fierce animal but if it runs into anyone it will probably get killed because people have been after him for many years but have never actually got him. He is a nice tiger but people think he is mean and horrible because of what he is. It is unfair but I guess it is true. He is a beast. The very next day he went during the day to a park and met a witch.

Archie Green (9)
Northlands Primary School And Nursery, Pitsea

Day In A Life Of A Pen

Dear Diary,

Today, I woke up on a wooden table. I was very confused due to the fact I couldn't do anything but roll. Suddenly, a group of kids walked through the door. I waited there, hoping I wouldn't be used. Until this one little kid picked me up and began to chew and throw me. Not even half a day in, a kid threw me across the room. At this point, I was agitated and my worst nightmare... I got squashed by a chair and thrown into a musty bin by an annoying child.

Skye Sayer (10)

Northlands Primary School And Nursery, Pitsea

Angry Tennis Ball Story

Suddenly, they started playing tennis with me. After a couple of hits, I went dizzy and shut my eyes until I was in Brazil and loving life in the tropical, humid rainforest. After a long nap, I went to get some fish and chips. Then I went to go to an ice cream shop and once I got my ice cream, I went to the lounge to sit with my wife Victoria. Lastly, while I was asleep, I got transported to Japan to play more tennis and go to Chinatown to get a fish with herby potatoes.

Clay Bainbridge (11)

Northlands Primary School And Nursery, Pitsea

The Teacher Turned Into A Monster

Dear Diary,

I thought it would be a normal day, but I was wrong. The teacher turned into a monster! She was a green, fat and ugly monster. Everyone screamed. All of a sudden, she ate Jim. My heart stopped as I looked behind me. I ran as fast as I could. I took my phone out and called for help but they didn't believe me. I had to save the world so I had to make a plan up. So I called my friends if they were alive. But they were. I was so happy. The plan's done.

Roman Oliver (10)

Northlands Primary School And Nursery, Pitsea

Puppy Witch

Dear Diary,

I was asleep and someone or something woke up from my puppy nap. I searched to look around for a clue and I found a letter with a biscuit inside. I read it and it said I was a witch and that I can go to a witch's school. I was so happy. I went to get my things so my owners wouldn't be in a hurry in the morning. When I finished I couldn't sleep because I was too excited.

In the morning, I was waiting for a car or a bus, but it was a broom!

Faith (10)

Northlands Primary School And Nursery, Pitsea

The Magical Rabbit

Once upon a time, there was a rabbit that was very different than his family and friends. He had a lightning scar on his back and he had magic powers. He could control the weather. That's why he is different. When he's mad, the weather turns into a thunderstorm. When he's crying, it rains. And when he's happy, there's a rainbow and it's sunny. Once, he found a farm, but it wasn't very sunny. He was the happiest rabbit in the whole entire world.

Gracie-Lee Read (10)
Northlands Primary School And Nursery, Pitsea

The Boy Who Wished

Dear Diary,

I woke up after a vivid dream about having superpowers. I saw a wishing star and wished it came true. The next day, I went to school and since no one liked me, I ate my lunch all alone. Some bullies came over and startled me. All of a sudden, I appeared back home and I thought I could teleport. I was so excited that I thought I could teleport. I was so excited that I thought I could fly, so I jumped off my roof and urgently fell. But I landed in my pool.

Jacob-James Sculley (10)

Northlands Primary School And Nursery, Pitsea

Amazing Football

Dear Diary,

I have been put in a bag for a week and I have to stay outside for an hour by the strongest kickers. Then the kids kick me. It really really hurts and when two people try to kick the back... ouch! It hurts more than the strongest kickers. I go super fast when I get kicked and get in the net. Also, it's horrible when I get kicked. I cry in pain and all the players that kick the ball. I roll away and they can never get me because I roll away. So bye.

Caleb Eastwood (10)
Northlands Primary School And Nursery, Pitsea

Day In The Life Of A Footballer

I woke up and got the opportunity to play for England. Then, I went to the training grounds to warm up. Although the star player, Stevan, was injured, I carried on playing and never gave up hope.

Match day, we started off with one goal and then I scored a scissor kick to win 2-0.

Day two, went to warm up and I did. Then I went to the pitch and five minutes in, I shot from the halfway line and scored. Everyone went mad. I won the World Cup for England.

Sid Butler (10)

Northlands Primary School And Nursery, Pitsea

GOAT Hydration

Dear Diary,

Today someone called Mbappé had a drink that was made by the two GOATs of football and had their fruit. He became so fast, running at sixty miles per hour and he was only two years old at the time!

I was so convinced that I paid a scammer one hundred US dollars to drink it. And then I drank it and shot my football so hard that the Earth exploded. And there was only one survivor and that was the GOAT, Messi, holding his World Cup.

Gabriel Atiase (10)

Northlands Primary School And Nursery, Pitsea

Am I Changing Into A Dog?

Dear Diary,

I was playing football on the field and a dog appeared from nowhere and he bit me on the leg. Then I saw my leg was changing. I rushed to hospital. Then the dog appeared again. This time, he bit me on the arm. After, a cat appeared. Now, the cat was hungry. I gave the cat some milk to drink and I changed back into a human again. The cat was a good cat. Then the cat started talking and the cat changed into a human!

Nikolas Tunase (9)

Northlands Primary School And Nursery, Pitsea

Sea Job With SpongeBob And Patrick

Dear Diary,

Today, I got a job working in the ocean and I saw some animals. I also saw SpongeBob, Patrick and Squidward. I had a really fun time and I collected lots of shells. I also found some rare fish. I called one Starfish (one looked like Patrick). I had a really fun time so I think I will do it again. I will get my job there one day but I will also do it every other weekend and I will have a fun time every time I go.

Casey Harding (10)

Northlands Primary School And Nursery, Pitsea

New Friend

Dear Diary,

Today I went to the beach with my dog and we went to get some yummy doughnuts. I sat and relaxed while my dog played around. I got up and went into the water and I met a nice lady. We had a good conversation. She asked if we could be friends and I said yes. We went round to her house and I had dinner and we went out because she needed to pick up her new dog at the adoption centre. We went home and went to bed.

Izzie Hibbitt

Northlands Primary School And Nursery, Pitsea

Golden Boot

This morning, there was a knock on my front door. As I opened the old, creaky door, there was no one there... but there was a cardboard box. I wondered who dropped it off. I placed it on the dirty table as a magical golden boot appeared saying, "You will score every goal." I couldn't believe this was true. When I got on my school team, I shot not on target but I curved it in like Messi winning the World Cup!

Ramsey McDala (10)
Northlands Primary School And Nursery, Pitsea

Spider

Dear Diary,
When I woke up, I felt different. I opened my eyes and I could see everywhere but I looked at myself and I was a spider! I could make webs, I could climb walls and see every movement and I only wanted a fly! So I made a web and I caught one. So I webbed it up and ate it. It was delicious. I guess that's my food now. I was good anyway, I caught another one. I ate him with glee. I loved it.

Jude Jones (10)
Northlands Primary School And Nursery, Pitsea

The Mystery Day

Dear Diary,

Today was a mystery day. Me and my best friend went on a walk to get some chocolate because we were hungry. Then we came across a strange person who was selling chocolate for free which was strange to do. But we were so curious to get it so my friend went alone to get it.

Next, we went back home. We looked around and inside the chocolate until we found a drug...

Catriel Heredia Aguiar (10)
Northlands Primary School And Nursery, Pitsea

The Girlfriend Incident

Once upon a time, there was a girl called Sailish and she had a crush on a popular boy called Nidal. He had a girlfriend called Joshella. Joshella was cheating on him with Brian so he is lonely.

"Hey Sailish, do you want to go to the disco with me?"

"Umm, okay."

"Wow, nice dress Sailish. I really like it!"

"Do you have a girlfriend?"

"No!"

"Oh."

"Can I ask you something?"

"Okay."

"Will you be my girlfriend please? I always look at you."

"Okay, I am so happy and you are my crush."

"Goodbye, night babe."

Fenella Lambert (11)

Shrewsbury Cathedral Catholic Primary School, Castlefields

The Incredible Diary

Once upon a time, there was a girl called Lilly. There was a diary. It wasn't just a normal diary. It was an incredible diary. In the diary, it said, 'I hate someone'. Lilly was trying to think about whose diary it was. Then she knew whose it was. It was Ianshed's diary. Lilly asked, "Why do you hate someone?"

He said, "What? I don't hate someone."

So whose diary is it? Then there was a tiger. The tiger was mean so the tiger chased Lilly. Lilly said, "Arghh!"

Then the tiger was nice. She petted the tiger. Lovely.

Liepa Petrenaite (7)
Shrewsbury Cathedral Catholic Primary School, Castlefields

The Reindeer And The Butterfly

Once upon a time, there was a reindeer sitting by a pond. There flew a butterfly. She was sad. She was lonely.

"I will play with you," said the reindeer. The butterfly showed where she lived.

"I live in a tree!"

"Let's play tag."

"Okay," said the butterfly.

One day, a woodpecker started to peck the tree.

"Oh no!" said the butterfly.

"Don't worry, you can live at my house. I live in the grassy fields."

"Thank you."

They all became a big happy family.

Lacee Beau Fairley (8)

Shrewsbury Cathedral Catholic Primary School, Castlefields

The Fairy Who Wanted To Make A Difference

Dear Diary,

This is Angelica Rose and I'm inspired to make a difference and here's why. I was heading into town when I stumbled across a door I didn't recognise. So I walked in and suddenly a big parade of noise arose and hundreds of people were walking the dirty streets while shouting something at a weird rectangular shape. Then I remembered, this is the place my mum told me about. The real NYC. It's sadder than the stories: dirty, gross and dead. I don't know how someone could live here but it gave me a new feeling.

Angelica.

Martha Reavey (11)

Shrewsbury Cathedral Catholic Primary School, Castlefields

Diary Of An Aggressive Girl

Dear Diary,
Today isn't a day like any other. My so-called mischievous sister is up to her tricks again. First, when she was baking muffins with my mum, she spilled the flour all over me which I'm certainly sure she did on purpose. Things at school aren't that great also. Spilling your food at lunch in front of the whole school and the school's biggest bully is pretty embarrassing you know. Living a life at home and in high school is pretty bad for me you know. Typically, my life's the worst life ever lived.

Oluwadamilola Grace Osewa (10)
Shrewsbury Cathedral Catholic Primary School, Castlefields

Ice Cream Farm Day

Dear Diary,

I was with my family when we went to the ice cream farm. First, we went on Marshmallow Mound. It was so much fun. My favourite ride was the soft play and my second favourite was Silvercone. It was racing cars. After, we played in different areas of the park. We tried different flavours of ice creams. The most delicious one was marshmallow ice cream. I enjoyed playing in the water, in the wet area of the park. Then we had some food. I had a hot dog. Also, we took lots of photos. We went back home.

Isabell Abraham (11)

Shrewsbury Cathedral Catholic Primary School, Castlefields

My Favourite Day

My favourite day is my eighth birthday. Early in the day, my mother threw a surprise party for me. She baked my favourite chocolate cake. I got a lot of presents. We had such fun playing exciting games. After lunch, my parents gave me a wonderful surprise gift. It was a beautiful doll. I named her Elsa. She is my best friend today. Later, my friend and I went to the zoo. We saw elephants. The zoo was so large. We walked for miles. Finally, we gave up and went home. Of all my birthdays, that was my favourite day.

Vimbai Mhembere (8)

Shrewsbury Cathedral Catholic Primary School, Castlefields

Jordern's Surprising Treasure

Dear Diary,

I am going to tell you my surprising treasure story. One day, I went under the sea to study sea creatures. There, I found a bottle with a map. First, I didn't realise it was a treasure map. Later, I looked carefully at the map and found it was a treasure map. The next day, I went on with the submarine and followed the map. It took me ten long hours to reach the destination. While on the way, I found the box with keys which unlocked the big rock and then I found the big treasure.

Ayansh Raneesh (7)
Shrewsbury Cathedral Catholic Primary School, Castlefields

My Special Day

Dear Diary,

I woke up just in time for church and I learned some good things. And after church, me and my sister cleaned the sitting room. And then we went to eat our breakfast which was strawberry bread and tea. But then my little sister showed up and she made the sitting room a mess. As for the result, she had to clean it herself.

At night, I watched TV and my baby sister was eating her dinner. After I finished, then we went to bed. I was really happy that today was a special day.

Oluwatimileyin Osewa (7)

Shrewsbury Cathedral Catholic Primary School, Castlefields

Monsters Are Just Like Humans

One day, there were three monsters, who had spiky fur eyes. They were sad because everyone was frightened of them until one day, they went into town. No one was there except one little boy called AJ. AJ took them to his house. One day, they played hide-and-seek and then... AJ looked around the house... They went missing!
"Oh no!" cried out AJ.
Luckily, about two hours later, AJ found them so they went to London to celebrate. At the end, it was all happy.

Jacob White (8)
Shrewsbury Cathedral Catholic Primary School, Castlefields

Journal Entry: 08/06/45 - End Of The World

They're all gone now, Every last person. Their lifeless bodies are scattered across the field like seeds. It's helpless now. All our hopes and dreams end up expired on these plains like the innocent souls who lie here. I *could* run back over that towering dejected border and get back to camp yet I don't want to. I shall at least look for my brother who selflessly volunteered for mankind - but failed miserably. I can see a dim red light flickering vigorously. They're back for more blood. Their stifling smoke alongside them. If you're reading this journal, you're too late...

Temidayo Oladipupo (11)

Southfields Primary School, Stanground

The Day I Discovered My Teacher's Secret

Friday 20th January

Dear Diary,

Oh my gosh! Guess what happened today? I went to school but my teacher was looking different. First, she was drinking something red and bubbly. She also roared when she was angry and something really weird happened too. She didn't want to go outside and she closed the blinds and kept hiding in the cupboard. I think she is a vampire!

Monday 23rd January

Dear Diary,

Actually, I was wrong. My teacher was sick and she was drinking cough syrup and she was blowing her nose in the cupboard! Silly me!

Talk later alligator.

Zayaan Hammad (5)

Southfields Primary School, Stanground

My Journey

Dear Diary,
Trauma consumed me as darkness lingered over me like a heavy weighted blanket or the monster under my bed. I'm living in nothing but fear, nothing but terror, nothing but chaos... Ever since that day, the war took my dad, my days have become deep, dark and depressing. And my fun also didn't last long, it went from happiness, joy, warmth and comfort to devastation. I can guarantee that my mother will never be the same. Life was bliss when Dad was here. I was his little princess, Daddy's girl.
Now the journey begins. My journey.
Love,
Aaliyah

Aisha Keita
Southfields Primary School, Stanground

My Designs

Dear Diary,

Today I became an artist and a researcher. I learned this design and that the phoenix is said to be incredibly strong, able to lift entire trees and fly for great distances. The mythical bird is also said to have the power of regeneration, able to heal itself from any wound.

Glichygodzilla/Glichy Mechagodzilla gains several abilities, including the ability to fire its arms off on a pair cables from its shoulders. In the first fight against Godzilla, Glichygodzilla overpowers him, tearing his dorsal fins and blasting his eyes with shots of his glichy cluster ray.

Mazin Elmahi (11)
Southfields Primary School, Stanground

The Unbelievable Day In The Life Of... Seetha!

Dear Diary,

Today was exciting! Our first subject was 'The Volcano of Colour'. You will not believe what happened, the volcano only erupts at night but today it erupted during class! My life flashed before my eyes. My heart was beating faster than ever because I thought we were about to die! Thankfully, the rescue team came in an explosion of smoke. They put spells on the volcano... but it didn't work. Everyone started panicking. As we started to lose hope, the one and only headmaster came to save us. And in one flick... we... were... saved!

Hanika Padmanabhan (9)

Southfields Primary School, Stanground

Egyptian Pyramid Dreams

Dear Diary,

I am always fascinated by deserts and pyramids. One day, I magically disappeared to a desert along with my friend named Joe. We suddenly felt so hot that I thought the temperature was above 100°F. First, we spotted two camels. Then we rode on these humpy creatures to the pyramids. Inside the pyramids, we were both scared while seeing the mummies and skeletons. On the other hand, we found chests of treasure that made us pretty excited. Out of curiosity, we tried to open a chest, but we realised it was an extraordinary dream.

Krithvik Sankaranarayanan (7)
Southfields Primary School, Stanground

The Top Secret Diary Of Geometric Gracie

Dear Diary,

I don't think I've ever experienced something like this in a very long time. It was 4:05am and my gadget watch was beside the bed. Without a sudden warning, my watch set off with an alert. It read, 'Gracie! We need your help! Urgently! Head over to Quad Lake Branch! Now!' I rubbed my eyes open. It was the first time ever that my geometric powers could possibly save the world! I grabbed my gear and slid on my super awesome green and blue boots. I crept out the door slowly. Indiana was in need of me.

Caris Isaac (10)

Southfields Primary School, Stanground

The Eventful Hurricane

Today was a very hectic day! It all commenced just as the school bell rang. As we entered the classroom, the most unpredictable thing happened. A roaring hurricane appeared, taking everything in its steps. The next morning, I woke up baffled and frustrated, not knowing where I was. I decided to explore and wondered where in the world I was. As I looked around, I realised that I was in Makkah. I was in awe of all of the beautiful sites. But the most beautiful (in my opinion) was the Kaaba. I never knew a hurricane could do so much!

Mariama Embalo (9)
Southfields Primary School, Stanground

My Secret Spot

Dear Diary,

I, the beautiful butterfly, flew high to collect nectar and pollinate, just like every day. Flying in-between the heavenly-smelling jasmine flowers was an exciting experience.

Later, I decided to taste the honey I had collected for the past few days. Unfortunately, my friend, the Monarch, spotted me licking my precious honey.

He instantly snatched it from me! What a disgrace! Luckily, I had another pot hidden in my blue pouch and enjoyed it in my secret hiding spot which I will not tell you my dear diary.

Yatika Prabhuram (7)

Southfields Primary School, Stanground

A Day In The Life Of The Sun

Dear Diary,
Today was another hot day in the universe. I stretched out my long, hot sun rays straight away. I spotted Earth in a different outfit. Firstly, I didn't realise something was off though. The outfit was browner than usual and it was worn out. I felt brokenhearted. Sadly, I knew that Earth would be worse and worse, but I couldn't do anything to help. Late in the evening, when the moon took my shift, I was wondering, *how could we all make the Earth a greener place?*
Well, goodnight.

Alex Ivanov (9)
Southfields Primary School, Stanground

Life With Emotion Matching Skin

Dear Diary,

As I am writing my first day, I will tell you about me. My name is Arisia and I go to Butterfly Garden Academy. When I'm happy, I turn yellow and when I'm sad, I'm blue. When I'm pink, my emotion is love and when I'm angry, I'm red. But I hide it with make-up. At school, I cried and I was exposed! I got scared and went under a table but I hoped that I wouldn't get tested. Everyone chuckled and my best friend screamed. I needed to close my eyes to calm me down and relax.

Briony Hill (8)

Southfields Primary School, Stanground

Bob Saves The Day

Bob, the fish, loves doing karate. When his owners fed the fish, Bob would do a front kick to the flakes. Mittons, the cat, wanted a fish dinner and sat on the side of the tank putting his paws in. Bob felt cross as his friends panicked. *Swoosh!* Kevin got caught by the cat's paw. "Bob! Help!" Bob thought quickly but the second paw arrived. "Watch out!" Then Bob did the best tornado kick and scared the cat, dropping Kevin back into the tank. "Wahoo! You saved the day Bob!"

James Logan (7)
Southfields Primary School, Stanground

A Farewell Match

Dear Diary,

It was the last game of my basketball career. My mentality was roaring but there was no fear inside of me. It would be one for the ages. Tip-off happened. We won the ball. I started dribbling and before I knew it, I was in the zone! There were masses of cheers and boos as I dominated the court. Loving the game for the last time. Drips of sweat trickled down my cheek, and aches and pains formed in my ankles. But I didn't give up the shot. The clock ticked as I fired my last three-pointer ever!

Oliver Traynor-England (11)
Southfields Primary School, Stanground

The Skiing Holiday

Dear Diary,

On Friday, I woke up tired and excited. We went to breakfast. I had Coco Pops with sugar. It was delicious. After breakfast, we all got dressed and went skiing for two hours. We got back from skiing and had lunch. After lunch, we went back to skiing. We got back and played in the snow and the bar. I love skiing. It's so fun! I had a chicken burger for dinner. At the disco, we danced to music, played games and drank mocktails. I showered, put on my pyjamas, read a story and then went to sleep.

Maisie Palmer (7)
Southfields Primary School, Stanground

Sharpening Lives

Dear Diary,

I am exhausted and tired of sharpening pencils. It's quite hard being a sharpener. I've been sharpening about twenty bright coloured pencils today. Some of them kept breaking hence I had to sharpen them all day long! Phew!

However, I know people sharpen pencils to draw pretty and cute drawings.

At last, I have a chance to rest with all my friends who are the most brightly coloured pencils in the world, inside the cosiest pencil case. Bright blue beauty is already snoring away!

Ratika Prabhuram (7)

Southfields Primary School, Stanground

The Secret Of Natalia

In Heaven, The Angel Guardian had to send one of the angels to Earth. Many hands were up. Almost everyone wanted to be that angel and then, our main character was chosen, Natalia. The Guardian agreed and let her down to Earth. After she landed, her halo and wings disappeared. Nobody had to know she was an angel. Her mission was to defeat the red dragon yet there was no dragon to be seen. the dragon was going to appear in the future so she had to live for a few years on this planet to protect all the citizens.

Wiktoria Nowak (11)
Southfields Primary School, Stanground

The Incredible Stone

Dear Diary,

I've had an amazing day, full of incredible times. I found a beautiful shiny stone full of magic. I ran to get my friend. We touched the stone and it gave us magic. Sienna had the power of flying and I had the power of turning people into frogs. We wanted to give the magic back to the stone because we felt horrible for all the other people. So we dug in the soil and it will never be seen again. Me and Sienna had an amazing experience but we wanted to be normal like everyone else.

Amelia Wlodarczak (8)
Southfields Primary School, Stanground

My Fantastic Cousin And My Great Dog

Dear Diary,

I have the best cousin in the world. I'm sad that we are not in the same class but we are in the same year group which is year two. One day, the teacher said to me and my class that we are going on a trip to Woburn Safari Park. When we arrived, I looked in the lion pen and it was my great amazing dog! Everyone looked at me and said, "Wow! Your dog is a beautiful colour!" I stayed and looked at my dog and said, "Kaira, come on. You need to come with me."

Poppy Whittington (6)
Southfields Primary School, Stanground

The Day Of Quool

Dear Diary,
Today it's the 109th of sweet peas and I'm going to a new school. It's called quool and it's the best quality. Oh, Mum's calling. It's time for quool. Okay, today was the best. I used a bubble gun, pea net and kitty grappler. I was top-notch, the highest in quool. I've got so many friends. At exercise time, we do triple jumps and galax stars. Oh no, I've got to go. Oh, what's going on? Arghh! Invaders. They're here.

Isobel Bishop (9)
Southfields Primary School, Stanground

The Prize Wand

Dear Diary,

Today, at school, I was just walking down the corridor when I found a trophy case that had the most beautiful wand I had ever seen in it. It had an entry sheet for a competition next to it. It also said the prize was the wand. The competition was that you had to make a diary entry. Here is my diary entry. I like this so I think I am going to continue with it. I have just received who won the competition and it is... Drumroll, please... Me!
Bye for now Diary.

Eila Reeves (8)
Southfields Primary School, Stanground

Beach Day

Dear Diary,
This day is beach day! Me and my friend (Melody) went to the beach. I couldn't wait! We needed towels, a bucket and spade, a beach umbrella and swimming costumes and then we went in the car and we were almost there. We saw you when we got there. We went on the beach. First, we had fish and chips. Next, we went in the sea. Last, we went on the rides. We had a great time but sadly it was time to head off.
Goodbye.

Brooke Bell (8)
Southfields Primary School, Stanground

YOUNG WRITERS INFORMATION

We hope you have enjoyed reading this book – and that you will continue to in the coming years.

If you're the parent or family member of an enthusiastic poet or story writer, do visit our website **www.youngwriters.co.uk/subscribe** and sign up to receive news, competitions, writing challenges and tips, activities and much, much more! There's lots to keep budding writers motivated!

If you would like to order further copies of this book, or any of our other titles, then please give us a call or order via your online account.

Young Writers
Remus House
Coltsfoot Drive
Peterborough
PE2 9BF
(01733) 890066
info@youngwriters.co.uk

Join in the conversation!
Tips, news, giveaways and much more!

 YoungWritersUK   YoungWritersCW   youngwriterscw

Scan to watch the
Incredible Diary Video

YoungWriters
— Est. 1991 —